# Readers love ANDREW GREY

## Artistic Appeal

"Mr. Grey's amazing storytelling ability captured this reader's attention from the first word and kept me enthralled with the story and the characters within the book until the very last word."

—Night Owl Reviews

## Artistic Pursuits

"…settle in for one entertaining ride."

—Love Romances and More

## A Troubled Range

"This is one book that I won't forget and you shouldn't miss it."

—Fallen Angels Reviews

## Helping of Love

"This story, like the others in the series, is a well-written, feel good story that I will be reading again."

—Literary Nymphs Reviews

## Legal Tender

"Buy the book and have an engaging, enjoyable day of reading."

—Randy's Book Bag Reviews

## Legal Artistry

"…a mix of old-fashioned romance and European flavour."

—Elisa Rolle Reviews and Ramblings

## A Foreign Range

"If you are looking for a quick romantic read about some emotionally guarded but hunky cowboys then saddle up and take a ride on the Range series."

—Guilty Indulgences

# THE
# GOOD
# FIGHT

## ANDREW GREY

*Dreamspinner Press*

Published by
Dreamspinner Press
5032 Capital Circle SW
Ste 2, PMB# 279
Tallahassee, FL 32305-7886
USA
http://www.dreamspinnerpress.com/

The Good Fight

Cover Art by Anne Cain
annecain.art@gmail.com

ISBN: 978-1-61372-736-2

Printed in the United States of America
First Edition
September 2012

eBook edition available
eBook ISBN: 978-1-61372-737-9

To all Native American peoples fighting for their heritage, their way of life, and their dignity.

CHAPTER

# ONE

"HELLO, Jerry," Peter said as he approached where I sat on the familiar bench in the small park across from Darrington's department store. This was sort of our spot, where we met for lunch once a week when the weather was good. When it wasn't, we met in Peter's small office in the store, but it was always nice to sit outside in the shade, even if it was hotter than hell. "You're a little early."

"I got finished with a project and thought I'd get down here before I got engrossed in another one," I told him as I stood up. Peter hugged the stuffing out of me, the same lunch bag he used every week still in his hand, probably momentarily forgotten in his enthusiastic greeting. I expected to feel it bump against my back, but it didn't for some reason. "How are things?" I asked once he stepped back, indicating the department store with my gaze.

"The same as usual. It's quiet this time of year," Peter answered, taking a seat on the bench, and I sat down as well. Darrington's was one of many department stores dying a slow death. It was still the place to shop in Sioux Falls, but a lot of the normal business that had once been there had migrated to the shopping centers on the south side of town near the Walmart and Lowe's. The place had been dying by inches for years, but somehow they'd managed to hold on, and that said a lot about the community and the people who worked there. Since meeting Peter a year earlier, I'd staunchly refused to shop anywhere else out of loyalty to Peter and because I liked the old place, with its ornate, gold-capped pillars that lined the main aisle and colorful tiled fountain in the center of the building. "You should stop by after lunch. We're having a huge sale on summer clothes," Peter said as he looked over my ensemble of jean shorts, old University of Wisconsin T-shirt, and flip-flops. "And God knows you could use the help."

"I like being comfortable," I protested. My job rarely required me to meet other people, or even leave my house, so I could dress the way I liked, and I was a hedonist for soft and comfy. I didn't give a damn how it looked as long as it felt good.

"You don't have to look like a street person," Peter countered as he lifted the lunch bag into his lap and opened it. A protest formed on my lips, but I looked down at myself and realized he was probably right. What I had on, especially compared with Peter's smart-looking work clothes, probably made it look as if he was having lunch with one of the homeless.

"Okay, after we're done eating, I'll come shopping with you," I promised, holding my hands up in surrender. "I didn't come here to be accosted by the clothes police," I added with a smile on my face, and Peter smacked my shoulder and chuckled before unzipping the top of the bag and pulling out a plastic container that he handed me. "What did Leonard make?" I asked, removing the top without waiting for an answer.

"Pineapple chicken salad," Peter answered with what sounded like anticipation as he handed me a fork and a round of pita bread. I reached for the bag by my feet and pulled out two bottles of iced tea that I'd gotten from a convenience store on my way over. "Leonard sends his love and told me to remind you about having dinner with us on Saturday."

"I'm looking forward to it," I told him honestly. My weekly lunches with Peter and the almost weekly dinners I was invited to were some of my only meals that didn't come out of a box and weren't eaten next to my computer. If I couldn't microwave it and forget it, I could give a crap about it when it came to food, but Leonard and Peter were trying to change that. Lately Leonard had taken to having me help him in the kitchen. He'd never said anything, but I knew he was trying to teach me the basics of cooking. "Can I bring something?" I asked with trepidation.

"Potatoes," Peter answered, and I had to stifle a gasp. Peter always says to bring a bottle of wine. I turned to check if he was serious, and he obviously was, because he continued eating as though he hadn't just dropped a cooking bombshell on me. "Leonard is serving steaks, so a simple potato salad would be perfect." There it was—that slight tremble round the mouth. Peter lifted his gaze, and his eyes caught mine. Setting his fork in the container, Peter threw his head back with a deep belly laugh. "Good God, you looked like I'd asked you to eat bugs," Peter gasped through peals of laughter. "You can just bring a bottle of wine. It'll probably be safer for everyone involved."

"No, you asked me to bring potatoes and I will," I told him defiantly, and Peter's laughter died as realization dawned on him. "Yes, you may be taking your lives into your own hands, but you're old and you've lived a good life, so you can go out with a bang, or a good case of botulism." It was my turn to chuckle, and Peter swatted my arm again, his laughter returning. "Besides, I can show Leonard how much I've learned." We returned to our lunch, and my gaze swept across the park with its gazebo, green grass, and huge trees with locusts singing in them.

"How's work?" Peter asked, and I swallowed my bite of heaven before sipping from my bottle of tea.

"Busy as hell. I did some checking this morning, and I have six months of work lined up, and that's if I work sixty hours a week. Otherwise I have nine months. It's good to be busy, but I'm turning away new clients who aren't able to get in line. I was doing that in San Francisco, as well, but in this economy, I hate to." Whenever I had to tell a potential client I couldn't get something done in their time frame, it killed me because I knew I'd probably never hear from them again. I'd always been afraid, ever since I went out on my own as a contract web systems designer, that the work would suddenly dry up and I'd end up trying to figure out a way to buy food. That, of course, hadn't happened. I knew that part of my success could be attributed to the way I'd always been able to get to what a client really wanted and needed. But that same part of me hated to see clients go to someone else, because I never wanted to disappoint them, even if I rarely actually met any of them. After all, I now lived in Sioux Falls, South Dakota, and many of the people I worked with were on either one coast or the other.

"I've been giving that some thought," Peter said, and I cringed slightly. This could not be good. Whenever Peter began thinking about something, it usually meant something along the lines of cough medicine when I was a kid. It might have been good for me, but it always tasted awful going down. "You should hire yourself some help," Peter said. "There are plenty of students who just graduated from the community college, and I bet there are some that are quite gifted."

I let his idea sink in, and it wasn't too bad. "I don't know anything about hiring people."

Peter scoffed. "Well, duh," he said, and I did a double take. Did he actually say that? "What do you think I do—twiddle my thumbs all day? I hire people. I am the director of Human Resources, after all." He looked haughty for a second, then chuckled. "I can help you weed out candidates and make sure you fill out all the right forms."

4

"Okay," I said doubtfully. "But will I be able to get as much done if I have to supervise other people?"

"I'm not talking about bringing on an army—one, maybe two people. You need to pass on what you know to others." Peter looked around the park at the nearly empty sidewalks. "This is South Dakota. It's a great place to live, affordable, with a decent quality of life, sort of. But we need to have more than the Black Hills, the Badlands, and the Corn Palace. You make a good living, and if you hired people, then they could too." Peter continued eating, talking almost continuously between bites. "You'll bill your clients at a reduced rate for your employees' services and check their work to make sure the quality is where you need it. I know you charge $120 an hour, so you charge less for their time, say a hundred an hour, and you pay them forty an hour, which for this area is an amazing wage. You make money not only on your time, but theirs as well." Peter set down the plastic container and turned to look at me. "You could work out a package for insurance, and that, along with the hourly wage, should attract the top talent. We could work out the details if you need some help, but this could turn into a great business." Peter's excitement was catching, and I found I was intrigued by the idea—not sold on it, but intrigued.

"How do I find qualified candidates? I don't want to put an ad in the paper and have a million people pestering me and sending me crap," I said, a bit surprised that I was pursuing this. But the idea had merit, I knew it did, and there had been times when I'd thought about hiring some help. I wasn't egotistical, but I also felt very strongly that I was among the best at what I did, and if quality suffered, then my livelihood would be out the door.

"Leave that to me. I can help you, and I won't waste your time with unqualified people. I can promise you that," Peter told me with determination, and I found myself agreeing.

"Am I going to have to find an office or something? I work out of my house, and I like it that way." I really did. I could fall out of bed, grab my coffee, and go to work in my underwear if I didn't feel like getting dressed. It didn't matter and I'd gotten quite used to it.

"Turn your grandfather's old workshop into an office," Peter suggested. "You'll never use the tools, and they're just sitting there. They may be old, but they're good quality. You could probably sell them easily, and you have one of those… radio Internet thingies." He waved his hand around the way he always did whenever he brought up anything technology related. "So everyone could work off it."

"Do you have someone who'd like the tools?" I knew exactly what Peter was thinking. "Why don't you tell Leonard that if he wants the tools, he can have them."

"We can't do that," Peter protested.

"Yes, you can. Grandpa would want those tools he used all those years to go to someone who will care for them and use them. He'd hate to have them sit and rust away, and so would I."

A cold feeling of loss settled into my heart as I thought of Grandpa and the last time I'd seen him working in his workshop. He'd said he was making something special at the time. A year earlier, I'd moved to Sioux Falls to take care of my mother's father. He was the only family I had left, at least as far as both they and I were concerned, and when he'd called and said he needed help, I'd packed up and moved back. Grandpa had lasted six months, and I took care of him and worked from his house. We got to know each other again, and after he died in his sleep, I realized how much I'd loved him and just how much time I'd lost. Grandpa had left me his house in his will, and I'd contemplated selling it and moving back to San Francisco, but by then I'd met Peter and Leonard, and consequently almost every other gay person in town, not that there were many, and they had convinced me to stay and put down roots. I hadn't regretted staying yet, although that could change, since I'd managed to avoid the rest of my family so far, except for the funeral, and the little town on the Great Plains had quickly become home.

"Leonard will be thrilled," Peter said, and I could feel his excitement. "But you know it isn't necessary."

"I know, and that's part of why I offered." Peter and Leonard had quickly grown into surrogate parents.

"So you'll consider hiring some help?" Peter verified, and I wondered what he was up to. "We worry about you working so much."

"You won't believe me, but I work fewer hours here than I did in San Francisco," I confessed. "The house itself takes a lot of time, and Grandpa left a lot of projects that need to be finished." Like the kitchen sink that only ran when it wanted to, or the back porch that needed the floor replaced. Mostly I hired people to do the work, but there were some things I liked to do myself to sort of get out of my head for a while. Not that it worked all that well, but a distraction from HTML and Java code was welcome and sometimes required to remain sane.

Peter didn't look as though he believed me, but he said nothing and began to close up his empty lunch container. I finished my salad and then handed him the Tupperware, and he put that away as well. Then I sat back on the bench and finished my tea. "Have you seen the falls since you got back?" he asked.

"Yeah. I always liked it there as a kid," I said, closing my eyes for a few seconds. "I used to like to lie on the grass and listen to the sound of the rushing water, and in the winter, the ice and cold always turned it into a magical sort of Christmas wonderland, especially with the colored lights." I could still remember the last time I was at the falls before I'd left town for good, or so I'd thought. I'd told my parents I was gay, and that had been that. I'd wanted to tell them earlier, but I'd been too

7

afraid and said nothing until I was done with college. I already had a job offer, and I'd told them a week before I'd planned to leave town. After the big news, I left earlier than anticipated and hadn't looked back or stayed in touch with anyone except Grandpa, who called me faithfully and had even flown out to California to see me a few times, and I'd shown him all around San Francisco....

"Jerry, are you still with me?" Peter's voice pulled me out of my daydream. "Where were you?"

"Just thinking of Grandpa, I'm sorry," I said guiltily. My mind tended to wander more and more lately. Sometimes, being back in town after so long, something unexpected would trigger a memory long suppressed or forgotten, and sometimes I'd remember something about Grandpa, the one person I could always count on for unconditional love. "You were saying," I prompted.

"Come on," Peter said as he stood up. "Let's take you shopping, and then you can go back home to your computers." Most of the time, I was more comfortable with the machines than I was with people. But I smiled and nodded as Peter led me across the street and into the air-conditioned store. "Jerry, this is Emile." Peter introduced me to a darkly handsome man as soon as we entered the menswear department. "He'll act as your personal shopper for the day." I rolled my eyes, but either Peter didn't see me or chose to ignore me. "Emile, he needs everything. This is how he usually dresses." Peter tsked before turning back to me. "You'll never catch a man looking like that. I know you don't judge on looks and you want someone willing to see the real you, but, honey, it never hurts to use a little bait on the hook." We were in Sioux Falls, and I really wanted to retort that I didn't think it mattered how much bait you used when there were no fish in the sea, but I kept quiet, and after saying good-bye to Peter, followed Emile through the department and let him "help" me pick out some new clothes. By the time he was done, my wallet was considerably lighter, but he'd assured me I would look good and had even written down what went with what, because I had no clue. The only thing I knew was not to mix stripes and plaids. I stopped by Peter's office to say good-bye before leaving the store and then schlepped my packages to my car and drove home.

My grandfather's house, because that was how I still thought of it, was on the edge of the city portion of town, as opposed to the suburban sprawl, such as it was. It wasn't particularly large, but it was one of the oldest homes in town, and Grandpa had always loved it. I parked the car, unloaded the packages, and then walked to the back door and let myself inside. After setting the bags in my bedroom, I immediately went to my computer to get to work, the list of things I had to get done growing longer by the minute.

THE following morning, I got up and showered before pulling on a pair of old shorts and another T-shirt. I did have some pride, after all, and wouldn't wear dirty clothes—unless I was desperate and forgot to do the laundry. I even unpacked my new clothes and put them in the washer. There was no way I could wear new clothes from the store without washing them and cutting out those tags they sewed inside the shirts. Those always drove me crazy. Anyway, after getting my cup of coffee, I settled at the computer to get to work.

At about ten, my phone rang. My first impulse was to ignore it and keep working. I was just beginning to solve one of the problems I'd been wrestling with all morning. "What?" I said absently as I answered the awful thing.

"Good morning to you too, sunshine," Peter said, and I sighed.

"Sorry. I'm in the middle of a problem on the code I'm supposed to deliver by the end of the day today, and I'm almost done. The damned thing is nearly perfect except for the loop that is determined to run one more time than it's supposed to, and I think I just found the answer, but then you called." All of that ran together in a blur of words and frustration.

"Take a deep breath and mark your place or whatever you do with that codey stuff." Peter gave me a second, and I made sure the line of code that I thought was the culprit had been highlighted. "I found you four people who might work well with you. When can you meet them?" Peter was speaking softly, and I knew he was at work and didn't want to be overheard.

"Already?" I said and then stopped. I knew I'd been had. There was no way Peter had just found these people. "How long have you been planning this?"

"Okay," Peter said with a chuckle, "you got me. I got a call from the community college because they have graduates who are having troubles finding jobs in the area. They're skilled and, from what I can tell, quite good. The problem is the brain drain. We have good colleges, but without the good jobs, they leave." He was such an activist, and I had to admit to myself that he was probably right.

"Fine, I'll meet with them tomorrow morning between ten and noon. I want résumés, and tell them each to bring me an application they've designed and coded themselves. I want to see examples of their work. I also want them to bring laptops if they have them, because they're going to have to code for me before I'll consider any of them." I figured I wasn't going to waste my time and effort on people who couldn't perform, and the best way to make sure of that was to make them prove it. That was how I'd gotten my first coding job.

Peter was quiet for a few seconds. "Is there anything more?" I figured Peter was writing things down.

"No. They can come to the house." I cradled the phone under my chin and resumed work, the error jumping out at me, and I changed the variable setting and reran the application. This time it worked perfectly. "Yes."

"Sorry?" Peter said.

"Nothing, I just fixed my error. Is there anything I need to have them fill out?"

"I'll bring you copies of the forms tonight. You'll need to make sure they sign them, and you should file them for records and legal purposes. You probably don't need them, because of the size of your business, but I want to be safe." Peter paused, and I assumed he was writing.

"Thanks, Peter. I'll have a martini waiting," I told him with a laugh. Peter always said I made the best martinis, but I didn't drink them so I had no idea if he was right. I made them the same way each time, though, so everybody was happy.

"It's a deal. I'll call Leonard and see if he wants to join us, and he can bring the truck and start to haul away the tools."

"Sounds good. I'll see you then." I hung up the phone and wondered just what I was getting myself into. I hadn't even agreed to hire someone else, and Peter had four people ready to come by for an interview. Not that it mattered, because I knew if none of them were acceptable, I wouldn't take them on, and if I got lucky and one of them happened to show promise, then I'd be a fool not to hire them and take off some of the pressure. Besides, I fully intended to take shameful advantage of Peter. If he was determined to busybody me into this, then he was going to have to help. Shaking my head to clear it, I moved my mouse to wake up the bank of computer screens and went back to work.

At some point during the day, I gulped down a sandwich and then went back to work. I was making amazing progress. The afternoon turned into one of those magic sets of hours when everything seemed to go right and the code flew from my fingers. I was in the zone and got an astounding amount of work done. By the time I heard the doorbell, I was so deep in what I was doing it barely registered. It wasn't until Peter tapped me on the shoulder that I actually looked up from my screens.

"I'm almost done here, can't stop or I'll lose it," I said, returning to my screens. My fingers continued flying over the keyboard until I had finished the draft of the program I was going to embed in the client's website database. This was going to be the heart of their system and would probably make them a lot of money. I knew they were going to love it. After pressing "save" on the computer, I backed away from the bank of monitors and blinked a few times to get used to the real world again. Spending hours in front on a monitor tended to make me a little blinky, and it always took a few seconds for my eyes to get accustomed to being away from the screens. "Sorry, Peter," I said, getting out of my comfy desk chair. "I'll mix up the martinis if you want to have a seat in the living room." I peered around. "Where's Leonard?"

"He's out in the workshop packing up some of the tools," Peter explained. "He'll be inside in a little bit. He said he'll load everything in the truck, and you can look it over before we leave just to make sure there isn't anything you wanted to keep."

"I already went through it and cleaned out the few things I wanted," I told him as I opened the cabinet in the dining room that contained the little bit of liquor I had. I pulled out the gin and vermouth before grabbing the pitcher. I started mixing, measuring the ingredients and pouring them over a lot of ice and then giving it a quick stir. Then, after putting three olives in each chilled glass, I poured the drinks. Peter took his glass and sipped from it as I heard the back door open, and Leonard joined us, like a moth to flame.

"Best martinis ever," Leonard said after taking a sip and clinking glasses with Peter. I got a diet soda, and we all sat in the living room. The furniture was still the same worn but comfortable chairs and sofa my grandmother had bought ages ago. I hadn't had time to replace anything, and frankly, I hadn't had the heart to do it, either. When I sat in the same chair my grandfather had used for years, it felt a bit like he was still here with me. "There were some unfinished projects your grandfather was working on," Leonard explained, setting his glass on the coffee table. "Do you want to keep them?"

I shook my head. "No. I'll never get around to finishing them, so if you'd like them, by all means take them. There's also some wood in there as well, and if you can use it, take that too." It was sad cleaning things out, but I knew it had to be done, and I could see Leonard's excitement, his blue eyes boggling like the proverbial kid in a candy store.

"There's a great collection of antique hand tools in the chests in the corner. I set those aside for you," Leonard said as he lifted his glass again. "They're too valuable to give away. I'd love them, but I can't take them. You should find a collector or antique dealer who can give you what they're worth."

"Thanks, Leonard, you and Peter are the best." I wasn't sure quite what to say. He could have taken everything and I wouldn't have known the difference. But that was the two of them—caring and as honest as anyone I'd ever met.

"We're here to help, you know that," Peter said softly, and I nodded. There were times when realization of all the time I'd wasted seemed to hit me hard. I'd been loved unconditionally by only one person in my life, and now he was gone. I'd spent years away because I hadn't known what he meant to me. Closing my eyes, I nodded once, trying to force the grief away as I once again realized how alone I was.

"Did you get everything set up for tomorrow?" I asked with a croak, desperately needing to change the subject.

"Yes," Peter answered. "I left the forms on the table in the dining room, and I scheduled the four appointments each for a half hour between ten and noon. Make sure they're prompt, and try your best to be nice. I know you're demanding, and you should be, but you can be respectful at the same time." Peter finished his drink and set down the glass. "I know you're not going to be mean or anything, but don't come off too strong, at least not right away."

I nodded, and once I got over being a bit pissed, I realized Peter was probably right. My first job interview in California had been grueling, and once it was over, I'd gotten the job, but I'd often wondered if it was worth it. "I'll make sure they talk more than I do, and I'll listen to what they have to say. I do plan to see what they can do, though."

"Of course. All I ask for is politeness, and for the record, what I'm telling you I tell everyone who interviews candidates at the store. Interviewing is an art, and if done right, you can bring out a lot of details." Peter stood up, and Leonard followed suit. I walked both of them out to their truck, and Leonard insisted I check the back. Then I hugged them both and waved as they pulled out of the drive. Sighing in the evening heat, I went back inside and was about to go back to work but decided I'd made plenty of progress, so instead I ordered a pizza and settled on the living room sofa for the evening.

THE following morning I got up early, showered, shaved, and dressed in some of my new clothes. I was on my third cup of coffee and already working when the doorbell rang. Feeling a little nervous, I walked through the house and opened the door. A young man stood on the front step, nervously bouncing from foot to foot, energy and excitement pouring out of every pore.

"Morning, I'm Bryce Morton," he said, shaking my hand vigorously. "You must be Mr. Lincoln; it's a pleasure to meet you." He smiled up at me, still shaking my hand. "Mr. Harmon said I was to be here promptly at ten." He actually checked his watch and then smiled back up at me.

"Please call me Jerry, and come in," I said as I took my hand back and motioned toward the dining room. "I work out of the house, and I'm in the process of creating a proper work space." At least the workshop was being cleaned out.

"No problem," Bryce said quickly, and I could hear the anticipation in his voice. "I Googled you after Mr. Harmon called and said he had set up the interview." Bryce set his case on the table. I took the chair across from him as Bryce continued talking, his blue eyes sparkling with interest, wisps of blond hair flopping in his eyes. "You've done some amazing work, and I can hardly believe you're here in Sioux Falls and that I might be able to work with you." Bryce smiled and his hands shook as he pulled out his chair and sat down. The kid was a bundle of energy, that was for sure.

"Did you bring a résumé?" I asked, and Bryce handed it to me before fishing out what looked like an older laptop from his bag. He pushed it off to the side, and I heard the beep as the machine booted up. Scanning the piece of paper, I noted a number of things, including that Bryce had a high GPA and had taken a number of computer-related classes. "Are you planning to go on for your bachelor's degree?" I asked, noting that he was graduating with his associate's degree.

Bryce stilled and some of his energy seemed to slip away. "Maybe someday," he answered, and I could tell by the regret in his eyes that he wanted to desperately. "I had a difficult enough time paying for community college. So until I can work and save up some money, I won't be able to go. It's only my mom, and she has two other kids still at home. They live outside Mitchell, so I've pretty much been on my own for the last two years." Bryce lifted his chin, and his eyes cleared. He might have been nervous, but he was also proud of what he'd accomplished so far. Checking his personal information, I saw that Bryce was twenty-two, and I figured he'd gone to school part time while he worked, judging by his work history.

"I understand. I worked my way through school as well," I told him before setting the résumé aside and grabbing the notepad I'd set out earlier. "I'd like you to tell me what it is about software development that you like." I'd found out a while ago that developing unique and vibrant systems took passion and excitement.

Bryce leaned forward in the chair. "You know when you get this puzzle that nobody else can solve? And you look at it for a while and then the answer comes to you? It's like that. There's nothing better than being given a problem or a situation and being able to puzzle and code your way out of it. The absolute bomb is being able to make a computer do something that no one else has done before. When I started school, I wanted to design and code video games because I loved the graphics, and maybe I will someday, but I realized in school that it's solving the problem, whatever it is, that's really cool."

"Okay," I said, feeling that jump in my stomach that I got when I was with another true techie. "Let's see what you can do." I reached into my pocket and handed him a thumb drive. "I have two folders on this drive. One is a full program that has something wrong with it. I want you to use the specifications that come with it to figure out what's wrong and fix it. The other folder is a set of specifications. I'd like you to develop the simple system from the specifications, using HTML." I handed the drive to him, and Bryce plugged it into his laptop. After copying the files, he disconnected it and handed it back.

"How much time do I have?" Bryce asked, and I could see him opening the files, his attention already being drawn away by the problem. That was a good sign, and I began to have a positive feeling about Bryce.

"I'd like your solutions by five o'clock today. You can work in the living room if you like." One of the things I was concerned about was the candidates having someone else help them. "I want you to solve the problems on your own, without help from anyone else." I really needed to see what each applicant could do on his own. What I'd given him wasn't particularly difficult, but it would test his ability to solve problems as well as help me determine his basic development skills. "Is there anything you'd like to ask me?"

"How much does the position pay?" Bryce asked, turning away from his computer screen to look me in the eye.

"Honestly, that depends upon your skill level." I felt a smile coming on as Bryce nodded his understanding. "I suspect a starting pay of eighteen to twenty dollars an hour, but that could go up quickly depending upon talent. I'm a consultant and get paid by the billable hour, and the more I can charge for your hours, the more you'll make. Personally, I don't care how much schooling you've had—if you have talent, you'll do well."

"Can I work from home?" Bryce asked.

"Maybe eventually, but not to start with," I answered, and Bryce had more questions about benefits and start times. He also asked about the equipment he would be working on, and I showed him my office. Bryce was definitely impressed. I made a note to myself to put together a list of equipment I would need to purchase for whomever I hired. We talked about benefits and working hours. His questions were good, and by the time he settled in one of the living room chairs with his computer on his lap, I had a pretty good feeling about him.

The doorbell rang with my next appointment, and I answered it. Another young man stood on the stoop, and I took him, and later the next young man, through the same interview process. I didn't get the same encouraging signals from them, but I gave them the problems. One of them gave up after fifteen minutes, and I thanked him for coming. He looked disappointed, but I thanked him anyway. The other interviewee admitted defeat just before the last interviewee arrived. I noticed that Bryce seemed lost in his computer, typing away as I escorted the third applicant outside. After shaking hands, I said good-bye and was about to close the front door when I saw a man striding up my walk toward the door. As he got closer, I felt my throat go dry, and I had to remind myself that this was a job interview and not a pickup at a Castro gay bar.

"I'm John Black Raven," he said with a smile, and we shook hands.

"Jerry Lincoln. I'm pleased to meet you." The heat from his hand was startling, and I had to tear my gaze away from John's deep, dark, almost black eyes. "Come in and we'll go into the dining room to talk." I motioned him inside, and John peered into the living room as we passed. I saw Bryce look up from his work, and he smiled and nodded to John, who did the same back before continuing on. "I take it you and Bryce know each other."

"Yes. We've had many classes together," John answered before pulling out a chair. He passed me his résumé, and I scanned it.

"Your grades are good, and you've had plenty of experience." It looked as though John had worked at least two jobs for years. Many of them appeared menial and looked like brutally hard, physical work. "None in software development," I commented. He was also older than the others, nearly twenty-seven.

"No. I worked hard to pay for school, and this is the first interview I've had." His eyes shone with intensity and determination, and I did my best not to look at John's shining black hair pulled into a ponytail, or his sun-kissed skin and full lips. This man was here for a job, and I needed to keep myself under control. "But I always work hard, and computers seem to speak to me."

I was intrigued. "How?"

"I seem to have a mind for them. My teachers often offered extra credit for solving tough problems, and I always saw the answers right away," John answered in a measured, rather soft-spoken tone that sounded almost musical. "I don't have much real-world experience because until I was able to come here to school, there were no opportunities." John sat back in the chair, indecision in his eyes, and I thought he wasn't going to elaborate. "I grew up on the reservation, and there are very few chances there." I'd heard rumors and stories, but I'd largely thought those were tales born out of narrow-minded stereotypes. "I left to try to make a better life," John added and then grew quiet. Of the four interviews, this one was definitely the hardest. Some things were apparent, though. John was a hard worker, and judging from his grades, that had transferred to his schoolwork.

"What sort of things would you like to know?" I asked him, and John asked the usual things about pay and benefits, which I answered the same as the others. I showed him my current workspace and explained about the work area that was being developed.

"Would the insurance also cover children?" John asked tentatively.

"You should be able to add them," I answered, reminding myself that I had to see about changing my health insurance policy if I was going to hire people. "How many children do you have?"

John looked sad. "None."

I thought his question combined with his answer odd, but it was really none of my business, so I let the subject drop. "I have something I'd like you to do for me so I can judge your skill level," I told John when we returned to the dining room. I handed him the thumb drive, and I watched as he pulled out a very old laptop. Then, after transferring the files, I got him settled in the living room.

"I'm finished," Bryce said with a grin once John was settled, and I had him come to the dining room to show me. Bryce had indeed found the error and fixed it. He'd also developed the application I'd requested. "I even got the exception handling to work with meaningful messages." Bryce showed me, and I couldn't help holding back a smile.

"It looks good," I said, quite pleased, because I had at least one candidate with potential. I made sure I had his current contact information, and after I shook Bryce's hand and said good-bye, he left with a grin on his face.

Once he was gone, I stopped in the living room again, and John looked up from his work. "Have you eaten?" I asked, and John nodded. "I'll be working. Come get me when you're done." John nodded again, and I sat down at my console to work. I could see John if I turned my head, and I found I was having trouble looking anywhere else. He was stunning, in a quiet, understated sort of way. His eyes held an intensity and pain that intrigued me, but it was his hair that I couldn't take my eyes off of, and I kept wondering what he'd look like with it loose around his expressive face. Forcing my attention to my work, I hid behind my monitors and got down to the task, but that failed as well. I kept wondering what I saw in John, and then I'd peer around the monitor again just to watch him for a few seconds.

I had lived in San Francisco and had seen smoking-hot men almost every day of my life—guys who walked down the street and made almost every head turn. Those men usually did nothing for me. Sure, they were pretty to look at and attractive as hell, but as soon as they opened their mouths, some form of incomprehensible gibberish came out with every other word punctuated by "like." "We, like, went to the store and, like, he grabbed my butt and I said, like, dude, like, don't do that." I'd actually heard that in a conversation, and I had wanted to smack the man on the side of the head. Somehow I knew deep down that John was very different from those men. There was definitely intelligence at the bottom of those eyes, and his attractiveness smoldered just below the surface in the way he walked and carried himself—tall and proud. I forced my eyes away from John and got to work for a while.

"I think I'm finished," John said as he got up from the sofa. Thankful for something to do besides stare at John, I got up and met him at the table. "I fixed the problem with the program; that was easy," John said. "But I wasn't sure quite what you wanted with your specifications. On the right, you said you wanted each of the graphics lined up with the appropriate links. I wasn't sure if you wanted them static or not, so I made them scroll." He brought up the page, and the graphics scrolled along the side of the screen from top to bottom. "If you click on the graphic, they can link to the other pages if you create them."

I smiled and stole a glance at John. "I was expecting the easy method, and instead you gave me more. Very good." I was more than a little impressed. He'd delivered something beyond what I had expected, and he'd done it in the same amount of time as Bryce. "I'll be making my decision in the next week."

"Thank you," John said, and we shook hands. Then he gathered his things, and I watched him leave. As soon as the door closed, I released a long sigh before walking into the kitchen. I grabbed a diet soda and chugged most of it as I ran over both viable candidates in my mind. After throwing the can in the recycling, I was about to return to work when the phone rang.

21

ANDREW GREY

I picked up the old house phone. "Hello," I answered, sitting at my workstation.

"Jerry, how did it go?" Peter asked excitedly. "I told you I could find qualified applicants, and I steered people your way I knew you could work with."

"How did you find these guys?" I asked, wondering how he'd been able to put together a group of reasonably qualified people so fast.

Peter sighed softly, and I heard him shifting as the phone crackled slightly. "Every summer there's a new graduating class, and at some point most of them don't get jobs and come here looking for anything so they can work. I simply pointed some of the more qualified people your way. I could have hired any of those men here at the store, but they'd either leave eventually or end up at a dead end. So what did you think?" Peter was not going to be put off.

"Two of them were fantastic, and I have to decide which of them I want to hire. They're both qualified, and I think I could work with either of them." I figured both Bryce and John would be a big help, and part of me had a particular preference, but I made it a point not to think with that head and make the right decisions for my business.

"Take some time and think about it. Your gut will tell you what you need to do," Peter said optimistically, and I rolled my eyes to the empty room.

"I'll do that," I promised, and after talking briefly about nothing, we hung up and I went back to work. I'd lost the better part of a day, and deadlines were always looming, so I hunkered down and tried not to think about red-brown skin, long black hair, and deep eyes. Getting into the code, I managed pretty well, and it wasn't until my stomach rumbled that I stopped and made some dinner. Leonard called while I was eating to ask if he could come pack up more of the tools, and I spent the evening helping him load them into the back of his truck. We made two trips that evening to his and Peter's house.

"Those are the boxes of antique tools, and that box is locked and I couldn't find the key, but it feels empty," Leonard explained as he showed me the things that he'd left, once we'd made the last trip. We moved all three wooden boxes into the attic, and I figured when I had a chance, I'd look for the key in among the myriad of keys Grandpa had kept. "This should make a nice office space," Leonard said as we cleaned and swept out the old workshop. The entire space smelled of fresh wood, a scent I knew I would always associate with Grandpa. After taking out the trash, I turned off the light and closed the workshop door, feeling a bit like I'd just left part of my grandfather behind.

"Are you okay, Jerry?" Leonard asked from behind me, and I nodded once, not ready to turn around because the emotions were too close to the surface. "You know it's okay to feel bad about letting his things go. That's normal, and so is moving on." I felt long, lanky arms pull me in, and then I was being hugged within an inch of my life. "You know that Peter and I love you to pieces, and we're here for anything you need." I knew that, but didn't answer, other than to return Leonard's hug and enjoy the feeling of being in someone's arms for a while. "It's okay," Leonard said, and I felt him rubbing my back lightly.

I completely lost track of how long we stood there in the backyard, but eventually Leonard released me, and we walked quietly to his truck. After saying good-bye and watching him drive away, I walked back into the empty house. Exhausted, I turned on the television and quickly fell asleep on the sofa. When I woke a few hours later, I went upstairs, cleaned up, and then climbed under the covers. As tired as I was, I figured I'd sleep soundly, but for most of the night I kept seeing and wondering about a particular face with dark eyes framed in glistening black hair. By the time I woke in the morning, I'd made up my mind regarding who I needed to hire.

CHAPTER

# TWO

"SO YOU'VE decided," Peter said a few days later as I sat in the cozy kitchen at his and Leonard's house. "Would you care to tell me which one you've decided to hire and why? Not that I'm here to change your mind, but sometimes it helps to voice important decisions."

I really wasn't sure how I could explain this to Peter, but I decided to give it a try. "Both Bryce and John are qualified, and when I gave them the project to complete, John went above and beyond."

"John is the Native American, correct?" Peter asked, and I nodded as his image flashed in my mind. I'd been trying for days, with no luck, to stop thinking about him. "Go on," Peter prompted.

"They both seem energetic and hardworking. Bryce has huge amounts of energy and reminds me of the Energizer Bunny. Once he gets started, he'll probably work until I force him to stop. John is a little older and more mature. He seems even-tempered and equally hardworking. It wasn't an easy decision to make."

"So, all things being equal, you chose John because he exceeded expectations. That's a good decision," Peter said, and I shook my head.

"I chose Bryce," I said, and Peter looked surprised. In fact, his expression bordered on shocked, but to his credit, he didn't say anything the way I expected him to. "I think we'll work better together." Peter continued looking at me, and if I hadn't known better, I'd have said he was undressing me with his eyes, and it was a bit unnerving.

"What's the real reason?" Peter asked as he continued to stare at me. "I'm not trying to influence your decision, but from what you just told me, the person you'll work best with is John, so what aren't you telling me?" I bit my lower lip, and Peter's lips softened and curved up into a smile. "I take it John is attractive."

"I can't stop thinking about him," I confessed. "He has these eyes and this hair and…. How am I supposed to work with him every day when I could barely take my eyes off him during the interview?" I didn't know how else to phrase what I was feeling. "When I'm working, I don't need distractions, and John is a huge distraction. It's not that I don't think he can do the job, because I believe he can, but I don't think I'll be able to do *my* job with him around." There, I'd said it, and Peter could yell at me if he wanted, but I was being honest.

"Well, thank God," Peter said as he lifted his martini glass. "Not that I agree with your logic, but we were beginning to think you were some sort of eunuch." Peter sipped his drink, peering over the glass. "You haven't dated at all in the year you've been here, and you never talk about anyone in San Francisco. I'm assuming you dated when you lived there."

"Of course I did," I snapped and reached for the martini Peter had made for Leonard, gulping from the glass. It took all my willpower to keep from coughing after I swallowed the strong liquor. Catching my breath, I drank the rest of the glass in a gulp, then set it back on the counter.

"I take it things didn't go well," Peter said with his infuriating ability as the god of understatement. "Do you want to talk about it?"

"No. I might be ready in a decade or two, but not now." I looked around for the usual pitcher, and Peter reached for it, moving it away.

"You don't need to drown your troubles. It doesn't help, trust me. You'll only wake up just as miserable *and* with a hangover. If you don't want to talk about what happened, then that's fine, but you know we'll be here if you want to talk."

"I know that. I just don't know when I'll be ready." I loved San Francisco, but there were people there and memories that I was more than happy to get away from, and Grandpa's request for help had been a great excuse. I had been able to help and reconnect with Grandpa while leaving behind some people along with some really stupid decisions.

"You aren't...." Peter began, and I saw him gulp from his glass, his eyes filling with concern, "... sick, are you?"

"No," I answered, and Peter's expression relaxed. "Let me say that sometimes things in San Francisco were too easy and too... readily available. Now let's please change the subject."

"Okay," Peter said, and Leonard came in the back door carrying a plate of chicken from the grill. "So when are you going to tell Bryce that he has the job?"

"I was going to call both Bryce and John tomorrow, and I'm hoping to spend the weekend turning the workshop into a rudimentary office."

"I'll help you," Leonard offered. "There's plenty of power, and your grandfather finished the walls and ceiling as well as insulated. All I can figure is that he worked out there all year long and realized if he wanted to work in the winter, he had to do something about heating. So all we need to do is clean them up good and paint, maybe replace the lights with something nicer than plain light strips, and you'll have a good place to add desks and things."

"I'd help too, but I need to work Saturday," Peter said, and I smiled.

"I appreciate everything both of you have done. So Saturday evening I'll take you both out for dinner." It was the least I could do. "You can pick the restaurant."

"Anywhere?" Peter asked, and I laughed as his eyes went wide.

"Yes, anywhere. You've had me over for so many meals and been so good to me, it's the least I can do. So pick the best restaurant in town, and we'll go Saturday night." It felt good to make plans to go out again. In San Francisco I had a lot of friends, and while I worked a lot, I had also found time to have fun. I hadn't done that much since I was here, and maybe it was time to change that. "Anyway, who knows, I may even go out on a date if I can find one of the four other gay men in town my age."

Peter scoffed. "There's at least six." And we all laughed and began carrying the food to the table.

As usual, dinner with Peter and Leonard was like being at home. We talked about the same sorts of things I imagined I'd talk to my parents about if they were still in my life. Sometimes that hurt, and I'd spent a lot of time when I was on the West Coast trying to forget. Peter talked about his day at work and worried about the future of the store. "I'm not sure how much longer we can hold on," Peter lamented, the way he usually did, and Leonard soothed him gently, just like always.

"It's going to be fine. The Fourth is coming up, and you know that always brings people into town," I told him. "Do you know if the store is doing that sidewalk sale like they did last year?" That got Peter excited, and he talked our ears off. Peter had worked at the Darrington's since he was in high school, and he'd worked his way up over the decades.

"Of course," Peter answered with an excited smile. "And for the first time in years I don't have to work that day," Peter said as he slipped his arm in Leonard's, "so we can spend the whole day together." The smile they shared warmed my heart. We continued eating, and afterward I helped clean up until Peter shooed me out of the kitchen. Leonard and I sat out back in the shade, watching the sun dip lower and soaking up the late-evening warmth as the heat of the day began to fade. Friends like this were worth their weight in gold.

THE following morning I went to my desk and picked up the phone. "Is Bryce there?" I asked. "This is Bryce," he said very fast, like he was about to jump out of his skin.

"This is Jerry Lincoln," I began.

"Did I get the job?" Bryce asked, and I couldn't stop myself from laughing.

"Yes, you did. Can you come in Monday morning? We can fill out paperwork and talk over your schedule and what I expect." I heard a whoop and I smiled. This had to be almost as good as Christmas morning. I remembered how it felt to get my first job, and I was fine listening to Bryce celebrate. "Bring your laptop, and we can set it up to work on the wireless network. I'll also have a computer for you to use."

"Will I get my own desk?" Bryce was just like a kid in the candy store.

"Yes, you will." *Provided I get the office area cleaned and set up.* But I fully planned on it. "I have work you can start on right away, so come ready and willing to get started." Another whoop followed, and he agreed to be at the house by eight o'clock. After hanging up, I put off making the phone call I'd been dreading, and instead, I walked to the kitchen for a cup of coffee. After bringing it back to my desk, I picked up the phone and heard someone talking.

"Jerry, is that you?"

"Hello?" I said in a hurry, thinking I recognized the voice.

"Yes, Jerry, it's Phil Grundauer."

"Hey, Phil," I said with a smile, leaning back in my chair. "How's business?" Phil was one of my best clients.

"Really good—too good." Phil always talked so fast I could barely understand him. "Look, I'll get to the point: we've decided to do that total web infrastructure upgrade you pitched to us last year, and we'd like you to design and construct all the customer-facing interfaces. We're going to do the work in four phases over six months. We're going to kick off next week, and we expect to have requirements and specifications to you in two months. Can you be ready to go then?" I swallowed hard and clamped my eyes closed, shaking my head. I'd pitched this idea to them a year ago when I was looking for work, and now that I had enough work to last for months already, they wanted to get started. "Jerry, are you there?"

"Yeah, I'm here. Look, I have plenty of work for the next three or four months. Can you start after that?" *I hope I hope.*

"They're pushing to start, now that the money has been allocated. I know it's short notice." He paused, and in my mind's eye, I could see Phil looking around his office like some cartoon character. "They'll pay a premium on your usual rate if you can start in two months, and since I know you'll probably need to hire some additional help, we'll even pay an advance against hours so you can ramp up."

That was too good to pass up, and my brain began to jump, trying to figure out how I could make this work. Phil was right—I did need more help. With six to nine months of work already waiting and then this job, I was going to be stretched very thin, even with Bryce's help. "All right. Send me the initial information and the request for proposal, along with the scope of the work you want us to do. You know the drill. I'll take a look at it and call you next week to finalize the basic parameters of the project." I couldn't believe I was agreeing to this, but the offer and money were too good to pass up.

"Very good. I'll get the information out to you, and we can finalize everything next week. Thanks, Jerry. You saved my butt on this one." Phil hung up, and I immediately wondered just what the hell I'd done.

There was no way I was ever going to meet all these commitments, even if I worked twelve-hour days for the next six months, and I probably would, no matter what. Leaning forward at my desk, I picked up John's resume and stared at it. I wasn't sure about surrounding myself with two rather inexperienced developers, but I didn't see where I had much choice. It wasn't as though this was California, where I could find experienced developers almost everywhere, and I'd pay through the nose. No, there was just one option open for me. So I picked up the phone.

Part of me was thrilled at the thought of seeing John again. His face, along with the imagined rest of him, had been playing a starring role in my dreams for days. As I began dialing the number, I reminded myself that I was being stupid. I had no idea if John was gay, and my fascination with him was completely immaterial. Pushing everything out of my mind except the task at hand, I dialed the number and listened for the ring.

"*Hau*," I heard a familiar, resonant voice say, and at first I wondered what I was hearing.

"Is John there, please?" I asked tentatively. I probably had the wrong number. I looked down at the résumé to make sure.

"This is John," he said calmly.

"John, this is Jerry Lincoln."

"Yes, I've been expecting your call." He sounded surprisingly subdued. "I heard from friends that Bryce got the job. It was nice of you to call, though. I do appreciate it." I made a note to keep in mind just how small this town was and how fast word got around. Everyone knew everyone, or knew someone who knew the people they didn't know. It seemed almost faster than the Internet.

"When you're working for me, you shouldn't make those kinds of assumptions." I stopped and waited for what I'd said to sink in. I heard a small gasp and then nothing more. "John, did you hear me?"

"You're offering me a job?" He sounded like he couldn't believe it.

"Yes. I have enough work right now to keep myself, Bryce, and you busy for months. So, yes, I've decided to hire both you and Bryce. I'd like you to be here Monday morning at eight, and bring your laptop." I told him the same things I'd told Bryce, and he readily agreed.

"Where will we all work?" John asked, and I explained to him about creating an office out of the workshop.

"I have some friends who are helping me finish it on Saturday." I was actually feeling excited about having a proper office instead of the rather makeshift location I'd set up in the house.

"Do you need help?" John asked, and it was his turn to surprise me. "I'm very good at building things." At first I thought he might have been offering because he thought it was the right thing to do, but he sounded energetic, and I found myself agreeing before I could second-guess myself.

"We're starting at nine," I told him, and he said he'd be there and then disconnected. My heart thumped in my chest at the thought of seeing John again. I knew I was being a bit of a fool, but I was looking forward to seeing him again. I should have gone back to work and gotten a start on the day, but instead I called Peter.

"I hired them both," I said, and I explained about the new job I'd gotten that morning. "I have enough work for at least eight months, maybe longer."

"What about your fascination with John?" Peter teased, and I could imagine his wicked smile.

"I'll deal with it," I answered. "I was probably being ridiculous, anyway. I only met him the one time, and I thought him attractive. It's not as though I can't control myself."

"I never said you couldn't," Peter agreed. "I'm pleased you hired both of them. I have a feeling that together they are going to be a huge asset to your business, and I doubt you're going to regret it." I heard Peter shifting around. "I'll talk to you at dinner tomorrow." Peter hung up, and I finally got to work, feeling damned good about what I'd decided.

BRIGHT and early Saturday morning, I was out at Lowe's buying paint and supplies to finish the office. Last night I'd come across a carpet store that had large, commercial carpet squares, and I figured we could use those to cover the concrete floor. I got back to the house at about eight thirty and was lugging everything into the new office space when Leonard drove up in his truck. "Morning," he called as he walked across the lawn carrying a travel coffee mug. "So, what do we need to do?" Leonard asked more to himself than to me as he stepped inside. "I see you got carpet, that's good. We can lay that once the paint dries. We should probably add baseboard moldings to finish the walls, but that can be done later. The main thing is to clean up and get the walls painted. Do you have the rest of the office furniture?"

"I bought two nice desks and chairs yesterday. They're being delivered later today," I explained.

"Then we'd better get started," Leonard said before setting his mug on the windowsill and grabbing the dust mop. We started with the ceiling and worked our way down. As we were sweeping up the floors, I heard a soft knock at the door. Turning, I saw John standing in the doorway in an old T-shirt and jeans.

"Can I help?" he asked tentatively, and I motioned him inside and made introductions.

"Leonard, this is John Black Raven. He's going to be working with me starting Monday. When I called him yesterday, he offered to help get the office ready." My throat went dry as I watched them shake hands. Then John stepped back and looked around without saying anything, looking a bit uncomfortable. "We're just about finished cleaning up, and then we can start painting."

"What was this place?" John asked. "What was this room used for?"

"It was my grandfather's workshop," I answered, watching as John moved through the room. He didn't answer, but eventually turned and smiled, and I felt a flutter in my stomach. Never in my life had I seen a simple smile transform a face from attractive to stunning, but John's certainly did.

"This will be a good place to work," he pronounced, and he immediately began helping Leonard spread the drop cloths. I wondered what that was about, but John seemed pleased, and I wasn't going to question it.

We opened and stirred the paint and then grabbed brushes and rollers. Leonard had the steady hand, and he volunteered to edge. I grabbed a brush as well and started in an opposite corner while John began to roll paint systematically on the walls. I wasn't really sure how productive I was, because I tended to watch John a lot more than I painted. His jeans hugged his hips, and each time he stretched upward to roll paint onto the ceiling, I caught a glimpse of a strip of rich copper flesh that drew my eye like a magnet, and when he was facing toward me, I got a peek of the sexy lines that formed just above his hips and led down into his jeans.

"You'll never get anything done if you keep watching him," Leonard whispered, and I saw him wink before he went back to work. I felt myself color and turned away from the object of my fascination and forced myself to work, which was difficult. We got the edging done, and then Leonard grabbed the other roller. It didn't take long for them to finish the first coat of paint, and with very little to do, I waited for them to finish. I felt a bit like a voyeur as I took in every fluid movement John made, and when he was turned away from me, I got the occasional view of his lower back. A small groan that nearly escaped brought me back to my senses.

"I'll be right back," I told them, and I headed toward the main portion of the house. The temperature had risen steadily during the day, so I grabbed cold drinks from the fridge, along with some snacks, before heading back to the workshop. They were just finishing up, and the room looked great. I'd decided to paint the walls off-white, and they glistened cleanly in the rays of sunshine that shone through the windows. I reminded myself that

I needed to get something to cover the windows or we were going to roast in the afternoons when the sun beat through them.

Leonard and John set their rollers aside once they were finished and took the cold sodas with grateful smiles. "The paint is drying pretty fast," Leonard commented, and I saw John nod. He hadn't talked much.

I retrieved some plastic bags to cover the brushes and rollers so they wouldn't dry out. "Why don't we get some lunch, and by the time we're done, we can probably put on the second coat of paint."

"Good idea," Leonard agreed, and I looked at John, who nodded. I closed the door, and Leonard led the way to his truck. I would have offered to drive, but it's one of Leonard's things. Peter said that in all the time he and Leonard had been together, he could count on one hand the number of times Leonard had let him drive when they went anywhere together.

"Sweet truck," John said as he climbed in and scooted over to the middle of the bench seat. I got in too and closed the door. The entire ride over to the diner, I listened as John and Leonard talked about trucks, engines, and horsepower. Thankfully, the conversation didn't continue once we reached the restaurant.

"Did you grow up on the reservation?" Leonard asked John, and he nodded.

"I couldn't stay, though," he answered softly. "Life there is hard, and I wanted... something more. I took all the work I could get and saved so I could go to school. I worked hard, and now I have a good job." John smiled at me, and I felt my heart skip a beat. I had to look away to keep from staring at him like a smitten teenager.

"What's the reservation like?" I asked, and I saw a cloud descend over John's face.

"Everyone knows everyone because we all grew up together. It's like an extended family of sorts, but very poor. There's high unemployment, and a lot of the people drink too much so they can forget. There isn't much opportunity, and that's why I left. Part of me didn't want to. My people have a rich and vibrant culture, and I love being a part of it. But I can't make a living there." The server approached, and we all gave her our orders. "Now I keep my peoples' ways in my heart as I make my own path."

From the look on John's face, I figured he'd appreciate a change of subject. "How did you get interested in computers?"

"I begged my mother for one, and she found an old one at a garage sale. It still worked, and I rebuilt it and saved my money so I could buy a better one. I always knew that I wanted to be the Bill Gates of my people." John turned to me. "I want to thank you for giving me a chance."

Now it was my turn to smile. "You earned it," I said, and I realized that I'd probably made the right decision the previous day. The server brought our drinks, and I tried to keep from squirming nervously in my seat. Every now and then John would brush up against me, and I wanted to reach out to stroke his arm just to see if his skin was as smooth and soft as it appeared. "The assignments I gave you weren't easy. Two applicants gave up and couldn't finish them. So you got the job based upon your ability, and you'll keep it based on your ability to learn and grow."

"Is that how you started?" John asked.

"My first job was at a technology company in California, where they were very demanding. I had to go through a much tougher screening process than I put you through. There were times when I nearly gave up, but I succeeded, and once I got the job, I made the most of it."

"How long did you stay there?"

"They went bankrupt a year after I started. They knew technology but had no idea how to run a business. But I learned a lot and moved on." John asked why I came to Sioux Falls, and I explained about my grandfather. "He was the only member of my family to accept me after I told them I was gay. I was raised extreme fundamentalist Christian, and they turned their backs on me."

"But they're your family," John said in disbelief.

"They believe what they do, and I can't change their minds. It's one of the things I've come to accept. My father's brother is the minister, and what he says is law as far as my family is concerned." The food arriving was a good opportunity to change the subject to something more pleasant, but that didn't seem to be in the cards.

"Did your family accept you?" Leonard asked John, and my interest in the plate in front of me dimmed considerably. Leonard had amazing gaydar, and sometimes he got to the heart of things without beating around the bush.

"Yes," John answered. "My culture views being gay differently than white culture… well, sort of. We're called two-spirits by some. But just being gay doesn't mean you're a two-spirit." John seemed to be having a tough time explaining. "It's very much a spiritual thing and hard to explain to outsiders. But to answer your question, most of my family understood. That can't be said for everyone in the tribe." John took a small bite from his sandwich. "How about your family? Did they understand?" John asked Leonard.

"I never told them. Peter and I come from a different era than you youngsters. I simply left Terre Haute after my stint in the army and never returned. My family had a lot in common with yours, Jerry, so I left to make my own way. I met Peter when I was passing through, and that was that. I did go back to visit, but always alone and never for very long. My relatives know

now, and some of them are supportive and some aren't, but I really don't give a rat's ass as long as I have Peter." Leonard leaned over the table as if he were sharing a secret. "Gay people have been making their own families forever, and sometimes they're the best kind." Leonard smiled at me, and I nodded in return.

For the rest of lunch, we talked about nothing in particular, and afterward we rode back to the house. The paint was dry, so we put a second coat on all the walls before cleaning everything up. I did my best not to watch John too closely and managed pretty well... most of the time. I kept telling myself that it didn't really matter because John was going to work for me, and that meant I needed to keep my hands and imagination at home, so to speak.

I had hoped to get the carpet laid, but the fumes were enough to make my head float, so I opened the windows to let in some air and shut the door once we'd removed all the supplies. We'd just finished when the doorbell rang and the men were there to deliver the furniture. I had them place it in the center of the room. After locking the door once again, I joined Leonard and John in the kitchen. "Thank you, John, you were a huge help," I told him.

"Do you want me to come over tomorrow to help finish it up?" John asked, and I was tempted to accept his offer.

"I should be able to lay the carpet and put up the new lighting, but thank you." I also had to get their workstations set up and mine moved out there, but I could do that as well. John smiled, and I went in search of my checkbook. I had no intention of letting John work all day for free, but when I tried to pay him, he shook his head defiantly and refused to take the check. "Thank you again, John. I'll see you Monday," I said as we walked toward the front door.

"You're welcome," John replied, and I watched as he left. After closing the door, I rejoined Leonard in the kitchen.

"You could have invited him to dinner," he said, finishing his drink. "You really are smitten with him, aren't you? And don't deny it, because I saw you watching every move he made all day long." Leonard smirked. "And don't think for a minute that you're the only one. He kept watching you too."

"He did?"

Leonard rolled his eyes. "No. The only reason he spent the day working on the office is because he gets off on paint fumes. That man is just as taken with you as you are with him." Leonard threw the soda can in the recycling.

"It doesn't matter, because he works for me," I said definitively.

Leonard scoffed lightly. "You're just using that as an excuse. Whatever happened to you before you came here has you hiding from any sort of relationship." Leonard held up his hands. "I'm not saying you should rush into anything, and you need to be careful, because he will be working for you, but don't dismiss him, either. There's a lot to that man, and if I were twenty years younger and didn't have Peter, I'd be interested in seeing what's hidden in the depths of those deep bedroom eyes." Leonard walked toward the door. "I'll see you in an hour at the restaurant." Without saying anything more, Leonard left, leaving me staring after him, wondering what the hell had just happened.

CHAPTER

# THREE

I BARELY slept Sunday night. My mind kept running over all the things I wanted to cover with Bryce and John. I'd managed to lay the carpet and get the desks and workstations set up. The paint hadn't been dry enough to hang the lighting until the previous evening, but I finally got that done as well. I even managed to find a network extender on a Sunday and got that hooked up. Everything was set and ready, except for me. I now had employees and people who were going to be relying on me for their livelihood. Up till now, that had only been me, but now it was two others as well. I'd made detailed lists of the tasks for each of them, and while I wasn't expecting them to be particularly productive on their first day, I did want them to get the feel for how things worked. Eventually, I gave up on sleep and wandered out into the new office by six. It still smelled a bit like paint, but most of the scent had dissipated. I'd placed an air conditioner in one of the windows, and it hummed softly. With all the equipment, I'd need to leave it on all the time during the summer to protect the computer hardware. I turned on my workstation and sat down to work.

There were two doors into the office area, one from the house and one from the outside. I'd probably been working for hours when I heard a knock on the outside door. When I got up to open the door, I realized I was standing in the middle of the office wearing only my underwear. The knock sounded again. "Just a minute," I called and raced for the door, thankful there were no windows in it. Unlocking it, I bounded for the door to the house. "Come in; I'll be right back," I called, and then I shut the door behind me. I raced through the house to my room and tugged on a pair of jeans and pulled on a T-shirt before hurrying back to the office. I stopped just outside the door and then opened it slowly. "Morning, guys," I said when I saw both of them looking at me.

"I told you he was in his underwear," Bryce said mischievously to John before turning to me. "Your shirt's on inside out." He snickered again, and John looked away as I pulled it off and turned it right side out before shrugging back into it.

"So, you two already know each other, that's good," I began, wanting to get the conversation off me and my underwear. "You can each take a desk. Those systems are set up on my network, and I've granted you permissions and set up space for your work." I showed them at the desk that Bryce had chosen. "I have an e-mail system, and you each have an address." I went on to explain how everything worked. "I have a first assignment for each of you waiting in your inbox. What I thought we'd do is get together at the end of each day to review progress and plan the next day." Both of them looked excited. "Your first assignments aren't too difficult, but they're part of a system that I'm putting together. We need to have this system developed, tested, and ready for delivery in three weeks."

"You mean we're working on real work?" Bryce asked.

"Yes, you are. This is work that a client is paying for, and that money allows me to give you a job, so I want you each to do your best." I sighed as I looked at both of them. "I wouldn't have hired either of you if I didn't think you could do the work," I added reassuringly. "If you have questions, ask, but please think about them before you do. I have work I have to get done as well."

"We understand," John said. "Is it okay if we talk things over together before we come to you?"

"Whatever you think," I answered, the problem I'd been working on when they arrived already calling to me. "I purposely placed your desks together. After lunch I'll show you both how to record your time. We bill each project and customer for each hour spent on their projects. What I want you both to do is bill between thirty-five and forty hours a week." As I said that, they settled at their respective desks, and I saw Bryce hunker down, click his mouse, and then he began keying, and I saw him reading. John also settled at his desk, but he seemed sort of in awe.

"This is mine?" John asked, looking up.

"To work on, yes. That's your PC, and you'll be the only one to use it," I explained.

"This is so cool," Bryce commented, and I peered at his monitor. He already had his application up and was starting on his assignment. I had them both working on basic system components, and I'd written detailed specifications for them so they could both get started. Peter had advised me to make sure I gave them both easy tasks that they could do and get a quick sense of accomplishment. He also said to have other tasks ready, so I had a list for each of them.

Bryce and John talked back and forth. Well, Bryce talked, and John answered questions. After a while, that dropped off too, and we all worked quietly. I sat at my desk and got to work as well. I had been worried I wouldn't be able to concentrate with John so close, but I didn't seem to be having that problem. However, I did catch myself peering over at him a few times, and once I saw him looking back.

I was still getting used to the new surroundings. I hadn't set a lunch period and was notorious for eating at my desk. When I got hungry, I went into the house to make a sandwich, and asked the guys if they wanted one as well. Bryce had brought a lunch, but John accepted, and I brought a plate and soda back for him. I also thought that a mini fridge out here would probably be an asset, so before returning to work I made a note to myself to get one. For a few minutes, I listened to the soft click of keyboards before returning to my task.

"I think I've got this done," Bryce told me toward the end of the day. I didn't get up from my desk, but looked between monitors.

"Make sure. We need to be efficient and accurate. Use the specifications I gave you like a checklist and verify every detail. Then try to break it. If you and John want to look at each other's work, that's fine, but when you give something to me or a customer to look at, make sure it's your best work." I knew Bryce was excited and wanted to prove himself, but speed wasn't as important as being right. Bryce returned to work. Soon I heard him working again, and I knew he'd found things he'd missed.

AT ABOUT five, I got up and wandered over to where they were both working. When I was in the middle of something I often worked into the evening, but I didn't expect them to do that. I also knew being disturbed when you were really cooking wasn't a good thing. My legs ached from sitting for so long, so I quietly left the office and wandered through the house to the front porch. Clouds were rolling in, and with the blocked sun, the temperature had fallen. I sat in one of the old chairs Grandpa had made years ago, closing my eyes to think. I heard the door open and close near me. "Are you and Bryce done for the day?" I asked without opening my eyes. Don't ask me how I knew it was John; I just did.

"Yes. He's shutting down his computer," John said, and I was about to get up when I heard what sounded like sniffles. Cracking my eyes open, I saw a kid in shorts and a T-shirt shuffling down the sidewalk, looking all around, sniffing.

"Mama," he called, and I watched as he continued walking closer to the house. "Mama," he called again. The sniffles got louder, and as he came closer I could see tears running down his cheeks. I stood up, walked down the steps, and went slowly out toward the sidewalk, where I knelt down in front of him as I heard thunder sound in the distance. I saw him jump. "Mama!" he yelled, and I touched his arm to calm him.

"What's wrong?" I asked him, looking into huge dark eyes and a dark, round face framed by jet-black hair. I heard the door of one of the neighbors' houses snap closed.

"That's one of them injun kids. Just leave him alone." I turned and glared at old Mr. Hooper, anger boiling inside me. He'd been a grouch and a certified pain in the ass for as long as I could remember, but this was the first time in my life that I contemplated hitting the old bastard. Instead I ignored him.

"Are you lost?" I asked him, and the kid sniffled and nodded. "What's your name?"

"Keyan," he answered, and I looked at John and then back at the boy.

"It's going to be all right. I'm Jerry and this is—" I was about to say "John" when he interrupted me.

"Akecheta," John said, and the boy sniffed once, and his eyes widened as if he were seeing John for the first time. Thunder sounded again, and the breeze, which had been blowing softly, picked up, whistling through the trees and around the house.

"Why don't you sit with us on the porch," I told Keyan. "Your mother is probably trying to find you." I figured she was probably looking frantically, and Keyan's wandering wasn't helping. If she didn't show up soon, I'd call the police. He nodded as lightning flashed, followed by more thunder. Keyan jumped and squeaked before hurrying up onto the porch. He stood near one of the front railings looking up and down the street, eyes scanning for his mother. Bryce came out, and I saw him and John talking before both of them sat down.

"You two can head home. I'll take care of things," I told them. Bryce peered toward the west, and I knew he was wondering whether he was going to get home before the storm hit. "Go on, Bryce. We'll review things in the morning." He nodded and said good night to both of us before hurrying to the driveway and into his car.

The first drops of rain hit the sidewalk as Bryce's taillights faded from view. The wind picked up, and I gently moved Keyan further back on the porch as the sky opened up. "I'd better call the police," I told John, and he placed his hand on my arm to stop me from going inside, shaking his head.

"Don't," John said. "She'll be here soon."

I was beginning to have doubts about that, but agreed to wait a few more minutes. As I was digging into my pocket for the phone, I heard a cry from the street, and the boy raced toward the edge of the porch. John stopped him, and a few seconds later a woman had the boy in her arms. He was crying, and she looked soaked to the skin as she rocked her son back and forth. "I've been looking for you everywhere," she scolded nervously before crushing him into a hug once more.

The rain came down harder, pounding the ground and pavement. "Please have a seat until the rain stops," I told her, and she nodded, sitting on one of the wooden chairs with her son close by.

45

"He wandered off and I've been looking for him all over," she explained, and I wanted to ask what had happened, but like any mother, she just seemed relieved to have found him. I turned to John and then went inside and returned with a towel that I handed to her. She dried her face and hands before handing the towel back.

"Thank you for the towel, and for helping Keyan," she said, and I took a minute to really look at her. She was a striking woman with pronounced cheekbones and huge eyes, with black hair pulled back into braids that hung down her back. She could have been a movie star, she was so striking.

"You're welcome. We found him fifteen minutes ago, and he'd just had a bit of a fright," I said, and she smiled, staring out into the rain. We didn't talk much, and when the rain let up, she lifted Keyan into her arms, and after saying thank you once again, she hurried off down the street.

"That was a nice thing you did. Thank you," John told me, and I turned to look at him, confused. "You helped her." John looked toward the neighboring porch where old man Hooper looked back at us. "Too many people are like him." John inclined his head, and I felt my righteous indignation rising.

"Dumb old fuck," I muttered. I usually don't swear, but I couldn't stop it this time. "John, do you mind if I ask a few questions? I don't mean anything by them, but they may not sound politically correct."

"You may ask anything," John said a bit warily. The rain picked up a bit, and the sky darkened once more. It was early evening, but it seemed later in the darkness.

"Is everyone from your tribe beautiful?" I realized how that sounded and shook my head. "Not that I've met many Native Americans, but the lady, her son… you." I knew I sounded like an idiot and wished I'd simply kept my mouth shut.

"You think I'm beautiful?" John asked, and I saw him move closer, a smile on his face, as I nodded. My heart beat a staccato rhythm in my chest, and John's rich scent mixed with the fresh smell of the rain. John moved still closer. "I think you're very handsome," John told me, our gazes meeting. I could have lost myself in the soul-deep eyes that stared back at me.

I shook my head slowly. "I'm pale and scrawny," I whispered, not wanting to break the spell his eyes held me under. "You're dark and strong." I wanted to touch and find out if his cheek was as soft and smooth as it looked and if his lips tasted as rich and earthy as the scent on his breath and the muskiness that flowed off him like the rainwater. I could feel my body being pulled toward him, my fantasies and longing overriding my brain. John drew closer, and I knew I shouldn't be doing this, but I wanted to kiss him more than anything.

"Did that injun kid find its mother?"

I backed away from John with a stifled groan and glared across at the other front porch. I could feel John tense next to me, like he was getting ready to launch himself at my neighbor. "You know, Mr. Hooper," I began calmly, "it's better to remain quiet and appear stupid than to open your mouth and remove all doubt!" By the end, my words snapped out of my mouth, and I think the old fart got the message, because he stood up, shaking, his eyes trying to burn a hole through me. With a grunt, he pulled open his front door and went inside, the screen slapping closed behind him. When I turned back to John, I caught a glimpse of a shocked look that quickly morphed into a smile.

The rain had largely stopped, and the sky continued to lighten with rays of sunshine already peeking through the clouds. "I should get going," John said, and I nodded, watching as he descended the steps. At the bottom, he stopped and turned. I waited, and he looked as though he were about to say something. He even parted his lips, but then turned and walked toward his car. "I'll see you in the morning," was all he said, and I nodded, watching him leave, curious about what had been on the tip of his tongue.

THE next two weeks were normal, or what I expected was the new normal. Bryce and John appeared to work well together, which I was extremely grateful for. John had begun to open up a little more, especially to Bryce, and they talked as they worked, which I tended to find a bit distracting, but since they weren't making mindless chatter, I learned to deal with it. There hadn't been any more near kisses, though part of me wished there had been, while the rest of me was grateful not to have the additional complication. Late Friday afternoon, I heard Bryce and John whispering back and forth at the other end of the office, and I peered through the monitors at them. "Something wrong?" I asked, and they both looked a bit guilty and shook their heads. Then I saw them each silently encouraging the other about something before settling back to work. "It's Friday, and you've both been working hard. So finish up and take off for the weekend and have a great fourth. I'll see you on Tuesday," I told them with a smile, figuring I'd answered their question. From the whispers and what sounded like hurried movements, I had.

"I'll see you, Jerry," Bryce called. "Have a good holiday."

"You too," I said happily. Peter and I had discussed it, and we'd put together a list of paid holidays. He'd also gotten me in touch with a lawyer, and we were in the process of incorporating my small but growing business. I continued working, and after about half an hour realized two things: one, that I wasn't alone, and two, that John wasn't working and seemed to be waiting for something. "Is there something wrong?" I asked lightly as I continued puzzling through a long set of statements to find what wasn't lining up.

"Can I speak with you?" John asked softly, even for him. I finished up what I was doing and then stood up, stretching high after sitting for so long. John's expression stopped me cold. Over the past two weeks, I'd gotten to know both him and Bryce fairly well. I knew when they were confused or overwhelmed by the look in their eyes. I'd also seen excitement and jubilation when they solved a difficult programming dilemma and got the correct results. But this was a new expression I'd never seen from John before—fear tinged with worry.

"Of course," I answered as a cold feeling took hold of my stomach. "Would you like to talk here or in the house?" He looked even more unsure of himself, so I motioned toward the door, figuring we might as well get comfortable, because I had a feeling this wasn't going to be quick. "What's on your mind?" I prompted once we were seated in the chairs in the living room.

"I need help," John began and then stopped like he wasn't sure where to begin. "Do you remember that boy we found out front a few weeks ago?"

"Yes."

"Did you wonder why I didn't want you to call the police?" John was getting at something, and I had to tamp down my usual impatience, which wasn't easy, and let him tell me what he wanted in his own time.

"Quite honestly, I thought I was getting impatient and you were asking for more time."

John shook his head. "I was afraid for the boy." John sighed. "This may be hard for you to understand, but I'll try to explain. I don't know if it's different in other places, but if you'd called the police and they'd found that little boy without his mother, they would have called child services."

"If his mother hadn't shown up, that would have been the right thing to do," I said.

49

"Not if you're Native American. How do I explain this." He sounded very frustrated. "The state tends to put Native kids into the foster-care system at the drop of a hat. We on the reservation call it the black hole." John moved to the edge of his seat and looked as agitated as I'd ever seen him. In fact, he looked more upset than I'd ever expected the rather stoic man to be. "Once a native kid enters foster care, they never come out. The state makes a lot of money on our children. The federal government pays more to the state for them to place special-needs children in foster care. The state gets six hundred dollars a month from the government for a normal child, but they get twelve hundred dollars for a special-needs child."

"Okay. I suppose that special-needs children are harder to place." I wasn't getting where John was going with this. "That, I understand."

"No, you don't. The state declared that all Native American children are special needs, so they get more money to house and feed them, to the tune of millions of dollars a year. So if you had called the police, they would have taken Keyan to child services, and his mother could fight for years and years to get him back, and child services would fight her all the way because of the money."

"That sounds far-fetched." John had to be exaggerating.

"It's not. South Dakota Child Services is one of the biggest agencies in the state, with a huge budget that they work hard to protect, and they do it at the expense of our children." John sounded almost pleading, and I wasn't sure what he wanted me to do.

"How do you know this?" I got the feeling he somehow knew from personal experience.

"My twin sister died six months ago in an accident. She wasn't married and had two children." John pulled out his wallet and showed me a picture of a boy about three and a little girl about five or six. "She named me their guardian, but I didn't have a job, and social services put them in foster care. They said I needed to have a steady job and a place to live. So I got an apartment and found a job. It was hard work and wasn't high paying, but I did it and went to school. The case worker, an ugly white woman, said I needed to arrange for child care. So I sent word to the tribe, and a number of women said they would take care of Mato and Ichante. I even got letters from them, but the agency wouldn't accept it and said I needed approved day care of family members to take care of them. The entire tribe is like family, but they wouldn't listen. My parents are too far away, and they aren't able to care for them or they would help."

I reached out and touched John's hand. "Is that why you asked about insurance during the interview?"

"Yes. I told the ugly white woman that I had a good job that offers insurance, and she asked for proof. So would you write a letter stating my salary and that you offer insurance that will cover the kids if I can get them?" He sounded a bit frantic.

"Of course. I'll have it for you when you come in to work on Tuesday. When is your appointment with her?"

"Thursday at nine. I hope that's okay?" John asked.

"Of course. You can make up the time you miss so you won't lose any pay, if you'd like. Is there anything else I can do?" I asked, and John shook his head. "When was the last time you saw them?"

"Five months ago. The foster parents said they don't want interference. But what they really want is to raise them like white people. The last time I saw them, they'd been given English names. He was Mike and she was suddenly Ione or something like that. They know very little about our culture or our ways, and if I can't get them back, they'll grow up knowing nothing at all about their heritage."

"When you see the case worker on Wednesday, tell her you want to visit them and you'll get a lawyer if you have to. Also, get her name and ask her to spell it. Make sure you write it down. Also, ask for the name of her supervisor, and if she asks, tell her you need to know who to name in the lawsuit and the proper information to give to the news media."

"How will that help?"

"She needs to be afraid of you, and government bureaucrats are deathly afraid of publicity. That can end a career, fast. Sometimes you just need to play the game a little. She knows she can't legally deny you access to your relatives, especially not when you're doing what you can to try to be able to provide for them. If you think it would help, I'll go with you."

"You'd do that?" John asked with disbelief.

"I love kids," I told him. "Of course I'll go with you, if it means you can see your niece and nephew. If the situations were reversed, I'd move heaven and earth to get my sister's children. I'd still do it, even though I haven't seen any of them in years. If they asked, I'd be there." I pushed away the old hurt because this wasn't about me.

"Thank you," John said, and he stood up to leave. "But I think I need to do this myself."

I slowly nodded my understanding. "Do you have holiday plans?" I asked, and John shook his head. "Peter, Leonard, and I are going to dinner and then fireworks on Sunday. You'd be welcome to join us if you like." I wasn't sure John would agree, but I didn't want him to spend the weekend alone.

"I don't want to intrude on your friends," John said.

"You wouldn't be. We always have a good time, and after dinner, Peter always fills Leonard and me with his desserts to the point neither of us can move. Then, after the fireworks, we all roll home. I'll call and check, but there's always so much, and I'd like you to come."

"Thank you," John replied as he walked toward the door. I wasn't sure if he was accepting or not and was about to ask when he added, "What time on Sunday?"

"We can meet here at four, and then we'll meet Peter and Leonard at the restaurant." John agreed, and I heard him leave the house, closing the door quietly behind him.

# CHAPTER
# FOUR

SUNDAY, I dressed comfortably, but I wanted to look nice as well. I knew that John was coming over, and while this wasn't a date—at least I kept telling myself it wasn't a date—I found I was going through all the nerves and anticipation of a first date, including trying on a million different things before settling on a simple pair of khaki shorts and a white shirt. By the time the doorbell rang, I had run myself nearly ragged. Hurrying down the stairs, I nearly tripped in my haste. Righting myself, I slowed down and opened the door. John looked amazing in dark shorts and an almost white shirt that made his skin seem richer against the pale fabric.

"Come in," I told him. "Would you like something to drink?"

"Soda or water, please," John said, and I closed the door behind him before walking to the kitchen. When I returned, I handed John the soda and then sat in the chair opposite him. I wasn't sure what to talk about. I knew work was safe, but we weren't working and that seemed out of place. I didn't want to ask about his niece and nephew. "Have you had a good weekend?" I knew it was lame, but staring silently at each other was a little unnerving.

"Yes. I caught up on some chores and read up on some programming techniques."

I chuckled. "Light reading." Thankfully, John got my sense of humor, and he laughed too. "I used to read all kinds of guides and programming language tutorials when I was starting out. You can't get everything you'll want to learn from a class, or even another programmer. Sometimes you have to go out on your own and just learn. I never took a class in web development; I learned on my own. College can give you the basics of logic, process, and even problem-solving, but they only touch on coding, and you have to really take it on yourself to learn it well."

"I figured that out by the end of the second day," John told me with a grin. "You challenged us right away, and that was amazing." John set his empty can on a coaster.

"Would you like something else? I have beer and the makings for martinis."

"No, thank you. I don't drink. On the reservation I've seen what alcohol can do, and I don't need that." John looked around the room. "It's not that I have anything against it. I'm just afraid that I might like it too much, so I stay away from it."

"I understand. I was the same way about smoking when I was in high school. I never tried it because I was afraid I might like it." I stood up and took the cans, throwing them in the recycling. "Peter and Leonard invited us over to their house for appetizers, so we should probably get going."

We left the house, and I drove to Peter and Leonard's. The entire drive over, I worried about the inevitable grilling I was going to get from Peter. Thankfully, he was a true gentleman, greeting John warmly and offering him a chair, a drink, and then immediately starting to ply him with food. It wasn't until John excused himself to go to the bathroom that the inquisition began.

"So what's going on with you two?" Peter asked as soon as John was out of earshot, and I immediately had flashbacks to high school.

"Nothing. He works for me, remember?" I answered.

Peter made an exaggerated roll of his head. "You never take your eyes off him, and he watches you all the time. You've been here fifteen minutes, and I bet you haven't looked away from each other for a grand total of two minutes."

"That may be so, but there's nothing happening," I responded softly. "He works for me, and I like him. He's smart and he laughs at my attempted jokes. But you know I can't do anything more. It wouldn't be right." I sounded like a broken record, and I knew I was starting to doubt my own convictions, because I wanted to explore things with John. "What if I did see where things led and it didn't work? I'd be jeopardizing my business as well as my heart, and what about Bryce? How would he feel if John and I were seeing each other?"

"Peter, stop pushing," Leonard said, coming to my aid.

I heard footsteps in the hall and immediately changed the subject. "What time are our reservations?" I needed a chance to think and get some distance from Peter's relationship kibitzing.

"We still have an hour," Peter answered, and the conversation turned to more normal subjects. It was funny, but I spent much of the next hour listening, and I learned some amazing things about John. John loved adventure stories as much as I did, and we'd read a lot of the same things. He also liked mysteries, and I offered to loan him some of my Dick Francis novels, while he agreed to loan me some of his Tony Hillerman books. We both loved movies with plenty of action and stuff that blew up. "I also like to work with my hands," John told Leonard, and the two of them talked for a while about woodworking until eventually they went out back to have a look at Leonard's shop. I helped Peter clean up, and by the time they returned, we needed to leave for the restaurant.

Peter had chosen a place we'd gone to often, and the hostess seated us at a table near the front windows. John and I ended up seated next to each other, by Peter's design, of course, and Peter kept the conversation lively and flowing throughout dinner. I found I kept looking at John, and he seemed to be having a good time. A few times he smiled at me, and my throat immediately went dry each time. Peter and Leonard were great hosts and they were very good at making everyone feel included in the conversation, including me, which could be a challenge sometimes. Especially when John would laugh about something, his resonant tone reverberating through me like a percussive hit.

"You actually considered joining the military?" Peter asked, pulling me out of my wandering thoughts.

"Yes. There aren't many opportunities on the reservation, and after high school I was about to do what a lot of younger guys did and join the military." John glanced in my direction. "I had met with the recruiter and had even brought home the forms I needed to fill out."

"What happened?" I asked quietly.

"I realized who I was and that I'd have to lie, and I didn't want to do that. I threw away the forms and stopped answering their telephone calls. Eventually, after the recruiter pestered me enough, I told him why I wasn't joining, and he left me alone. It wasn't long after that I told my family I was gay."

"How did they take it?"

John glanced over at me before answering, "As well as can be expected, I guess."

He'd already told me about his experience, and I zoned out slightly, watching his lips move and the way his throat bobbed when he swallowed. From where I sat, I could see the divot at the base of his neck, and I began to wonder what his skin would taste like. Every now and then, I would get a slight whiff of his scent, and I had to stop myself from moving closer just to smell him.

"My mother wanted me to go on a spirit quest."

I pulled myself out of my wanderings. "Did you?" The idea fascinated me.

"Yes. It was a very enlightening experience and helped me focus on what was really important in my life." John reached for his water glass and took a gulp before setting it back on the table. I think we all expected him to continue, but he sat quietly, and the conversation moved on.

After dinner, we drove to the park and placed blankets on the ground while Peter opened the basket he'd brought, and we had dessert while we waited. As darkness fell, I saw Peter and Leonard cautiously take each other's hands as they sat together on the blanket. The sky continued to darken, and children played around us with glow sticks and wands that flickered and flashed, all accompanied by multiple conversations, tons of anticipatory laughter, and screams of delight.

Then a single shell burst into the night, shattering the darkness as every voice quieted all at once. I felt John move a little closer. Another huge shell shot into the sky, bursting into a massive chrysanthemum of fire, followed by another, and then another. I felt John's hand on mine, and at first I thought it might have been an accident, but it came again. Turning my hand over, I felt his fingers intertwine with mine. I continued watching the fireworks, but my attention focused solely on where John's hand met mine, the warmth of his touch, the slight roughness from his hands. It was like my entire being concentrated on where my hand caressed his. I know it sounds a bit stupid and over

# THE GOOD FIGHT

dramatic, but that's how it felt—surprisingly innocent and intimate at the same time. There were families all around us who would probably move away if they saw this simple gesture, and maybe that was what made it seem so special. I'd had sex with other men and I'd had boyfriends of a sort, but this seemed… more. We were just holding hands, and it was probably my imagination, but the gesture felt significant.

The fireworks began to burst faster, coming closer together as the pace of the show sped up. I could feel John's fingers tighten around mine, and I turned slightly as a shell burst, the flash lighting John's face and illuminating his wide, bright smile. I smiled as well, tightening my own grip on his hand as the show reached its crescendo. Every other eye was on the sky, but I watched as the light played off John's skin. I saw him turn toward me and then move closer. Everything and everyone around me faded away, the booming of percussive shells fading into the background as John moved his face closer to mine. The ground shook at the end, and for a second I thought it was my heart.

The entire world became silent as the echo of the last shell faded away. People yelled and clapped, even whistled their delight. Then they began to move, and I turned my gaze away from John's eyes, and his hand slipped from mine as everyone began to stand up and gather their things. We did the same, following the crowd as it filtered out of the park and back toward the legions of parked cars.

John and I rode in the back of Peter's car to their house, and after saying good night, I drove John back to my place. After I pulled into the drive, I turned off the engine and sat in the car without moving. I didn't want this evening to end. "Would you like something to drink?"

John hesitated for a second. "That would be nice."

The evening was still warm, but the air felt fresh and comfortable. Some summer nights could feel like you were in a

59

sauna, but this one felt dry, so I brought the drinks outside. When I returned to the porch, I saw John sitting in my grandfather's old porch swing. As a kid, I'd loved that seat. I handed John his drink, then sat next to him, not sure if I should take his hand or not, but he answered that question for me when he took my hand.

"What are you thinking about?" I asked when John said nothing.

"Mato and Ichante," he said, and I felt John squeeze my hand slightly. "They would have loved seeing the fireworks, and I could have bought them glow sticks like the other people did." John stopped the swing from moving and turned toward me. "I often wonder what they're doing and if they're being treated well. The ugly white woman says they are, but I know she lies sometimes. I can see it in the way her eyes move." John began swinging again. "I'm going to insist on seeing them when I see her."

"Good," I said, and we sat quietly, swinging back and forth, holding hands. I couldn't remember the last time I'd sat with someone and was just glad they were there without conversation of some type. I finished my soda and set the can aside. I didn't want to move for fear our hands would slip apart. "Does your tribe have traditional children's toys?" I asked John, and I felt him shift on the seat.

"Of course," he answered. "I have an uncle who carves horses out of wood, and an aunt who makes dolls in the old ways. They aren't my real relatives, but I think you understand. Why?"

"I suggest you bring a gift when you visit," I said, turning to meet his gaze. "Have something of their heritage to give them. The foster parents can't object to you having a toy for them."

John nodded and smiled. "Thanks for being so understanding." I saw him moving closer once again, and this time I wasn't taking any chances. Letting go of John's hand, I brought mine to his cheek, stroking the skin lightly, moving him closer.

Our lips touched tentatively at first. John tasted like the wind and smelled like the prairie. His lips were both soft and firm as I nibbled on them lightly, and I heard a soft moan. The kiss deepened, and I felt John's lips part. I took advantage, sliding my tongue between them, tasting him fully. I cradled the back of his neck in my hand, holding him as I devoured his mouth. There was no way I could get enough of him in a single kiss, but I was certainly trying. My fears and doubts, so pronounced earlier in the evening, were nowhere in evidence, probably because I could feel the blood in my head racing south as my cock went instantly hard.

I heard another small moan and felt John moving closer. Darkness cloaked us as we continued our frantic kissing. For a brief second when we separated to breathe, I wished we were someplace more comfortable and conducive for this type of activity. But as soon as John kissed me again, thoughts of everything but him flew from my head. I curled my arms around him, pulling him tight to my body. I could feel him quiver with an excitement that seemed to mirror my own. The bench swing was unusually long, and I pressed John down onto the cushions, feeling him shift under me. I knew his legs were hanging off the swing, but it didn't seem to bother John, if the intensity of his kisses and the way he held me in his tight embrace were any indication.

Giving John's lips a break, I kissed my way along his neck, burying my nose in his skin. He tasted and smelled just like I thought he would: rich, musky, and all male. When I licked the base of his neck, I felt John squirm and then groan deep and long. There were so many things I wanted to do, and my mind, what little of it was still functioning, was nearly completely clouded by passionate lust. I wanted John more intensely than I'd ever wanted anyone in my life. But deep in my brain, some semblance of reason sparked to life, and I returned to his lips, kissing John hard one last time before slowly gentling the kisses.

Our lips parted and I tried to look into his eyes but could see very little in the darkness. Slowly, I stood up, stepping away so John could sit up, and then I sat next to him once again. I felt John lean against me, his head resting on my shoulder. We didn't talk for a long time. I put one arm around him and held John close as we slowly rocked back and forth in the swing. I had no idea how long we sat like that. It could have been ten minutes or half the night. Eventually I felt John shift. Standing up, I helped him to his feet, and John walked toward the porch steps. "Thank you for a memorable evening," he whispered, and I leaned in to give him one more kiss. When we parted, John said good night, and then I felt him move away. I watched him descend the stairs and then walk to his car. Then I went inside.

THE following morning, the one I'd given John and Bryce as a holiday, I spent much of the day working, or at least trying to work. My mind kept returning to the kiss that had knocked my socks off. At some point, I asked myself if it had been a mistake, but there was no way. Every time I thought about it, I felt myself smile. I was still concerned about mixing work and my private life. Besides, I kept telling myself it was only a kiss—a great kiss, but just a kiss. That didn't necessarily mean that John felt the same way I did or that he'd felt the same thing. So I spent much of Monday working and thinking about what had happened the evening before. When I had mulled it over for the millionth time, I was finally able to get it out of my mind. Only then was I able to get some work done, and once I got started, I didn't stop until my stomach growled that I'd missed dinner. After finishing up, I made something to eat, and then went to bed.

Tuesday, I got up early and was in the office as the sun began shining through the windows. I spent most of the time planning the week and making sure Bryce and John had their assignments for the week in their inboxes. I also checked the status of all the projects and deadlines I'd made to make sure I could meet the commitments. John was the first to arrive, and he said good morning happily before going right to his desk and getting to work.

"I have the letter you asked for," I said, and I grabbed the piece of paper off the printer, signed it, and then walked to John's desk.

"Thank you," John said, looking at the door and then back at me. "I...," John started and then stopped. "I know I should say something about the other night, but I don't know what."

"Just say what you feel," I said with a hopeful smile before continuing. "I don't regret what happened at all."

"I don't, either, but I'm worried that it may affect us working together. This job is important to me, and I really like it. I also like you, and... that kiss... and...." John nibbled enticingly on his lower lip.

I felt myself grinning, because a kiss I'd given him almost two days earlier still had the ability to fluster him. "Okay. We need to keep it professional when we're working, and as for the rest, let's take it one step at a time."

John's expression darkened slightly as he nodded. "Don't treat me any different than you do Bryce. He's a good guy."

"I promise." I had no intention of changing the way I treated either of them at work, regardless of what happened between John and me. I still felt this situation was fraught with pitfalls, but I found I wanted to explore things with John, and I was willing to take the risk if he was. "So, as your boss, get to work," I quipped with a wink, and he chuckled before settling at his computer.

63

I went back to work feeling a bit like I'd won the lottery. Eventually I heard Bryce come in and say good morning. I grunted something in return. John must have done the same thing, because I heard Bryce settle in his chair and comment in a stage whisper, "Careful or you'll turn into him." That got him another growl as I continued working to finalize an application for customer delivery.

The rest of the workday was normal, and I found that I could concentrate. The three of us had lunch together in the kitchen, joking and laughing, as usual. Toward the end of each day, I'd gotten into the habit of checking over the work that John and Bryce had finished for completeness and accuracy. "Bryce," I called lightly, and he walked over to my workstation. "You've got some errors here." I pointed them out and guided him in how to fix them. "This is the third time you've made this same error." I tried not to sound frustrated, but it was hard. I had to remind myself that both John and Bryce were young and learning. "Try slowing down a little. You're catching the hard stuff but missing some of the easier things, probably because of speed."

Bryce opened his mouth, probably to offer an excuse, but then snapped it closed again.

"Let me ask you this: If you were the customer, would you want to be given this?" I asked, and Bryce thought for a few moments and then shook his head. "Then always make sure your work is something you'd be willing to present to a client. Now, the good news is that you appear to have intricate logic correct, so fix these up and send it over. Once John finishes his last piece, we'll put this together and run it through a final test."

"I'm sorry, Jerry," Bryce said, but I stopped him.

"There's nothing to be sorry for," I said loudly enough for John to hear as well. "We're a team, and there will be times when we all make mistakes, including me. The important thing is to learn from our mistakes," I emphasized to Bryce. "And to make this interesting, first one of you to find one of my errors will get fifty bucks." Bryce hurried back to his desk, and I saw him get right to work. I looked at my e-mail to check on John's progress and saw a note telling me to disregard what he'd sent. He was retesting it. When John did send me his application, I found a few minor mistakes and pointed them out so he could fix them.

At the end of the day, I was exhausted and shut down my equipment when the guys did before closing the office and heading into the house. Bryce said his good-byes and left, while John followed me inside and sat in one of the kitchen chairs. "You look like you've got something on your mind," I prompted before grabbing two sodas out of the refrigerator.

"No. I'm just a little nervous, I guess."

I couldn't stop a laugh. "Join the club."

"Have you been out with a lot of other guys?" John asked me before sipping from his can.

"You could say that. I lived in San Francisco for quite a while, and there's everything there. When I first moved there, I fucked a lot of guys, but they didn't mean anything. Eventually I started dating, and I met a few nice guys."

"Was it hard to leave San Francisco" John asked.

"Yes and no," I answered. I wasn't sure I was ready to talk about the situation I'd left in San Francisco just yet, so I hedged. "It was hard to leave the city, but I guess I was sort of ready to, because after Grandpa died, I decided to stay here. Last winter was hard to endure, I can tell you that, but otherwise it's been pretty good."

"Did you leave someone behind?" John bit his lip the way I'd noticed he did when he was nervous.

"Not really." I walked around the counter and sat in the stool across from John. "Things in San Francisco can be really easy. I had a good technology job, and I spent a lot of time partying. That led me to try a lot of different things in the name of fun and letting off steam. Basically, I was stupid and I began to get in over my head. Then I met Brad, and he had his act together and helped me get straightened out. He was the one who convinced me to go out on my own." I missed him every day, but I didn't tell John that.

"Did you love him?" John asked, and I nodded.

"Yes, but more like an older brother. He wasn't a lover, but one of the best friends I ever had. About three months before I left, he died of AIDS. He'd gotten it from drug use and didn't find out he was infected until he'd managed to kick them." I could still see his earnest expression when he'd sat me down and explained the facts of life as he saw them. "Brad scared the shit out of me and showed me what could happen to me if I didn't clean up, and I did it more for him than me at first." I cradled the soda can in my hands nervously. "I haven't talked about this with anyone." To John's credit, he sat quietly and listened. "After Brad's death, I fell back into some of my old habits, but I stayed away from the drugs. Thank God." I continued fidgeting with the can, and John placed his hand on mine.

"You don't have to talk if you're not ready," John told me lightly.

"I got messed up with some people I should have stayed away from," I began, and I wondered why I was going into this. "I was at one of the clubs in town, really expensive, with smoking-hot guys. I sort of felt out of place, but when Carlos approached me and asked me to dance, I thought it was nice. Most guys at these places are there to hook up, but he treated me nice and even escorted me home. He showed up the next day with an offer to take me to dinner, which he did. For a month, my life became work and Carlos, and I fell for him in a big enough way that I was blind to everything around me." I sighed softly, remembering what a fool I was. "We spent all our time together, and he was better than any drug I'd ever taken. I thought he really cared for me, but then he started giving me computer programs to work on, and I quickly realized they were security programs and he wanted me to crack them." I started to shake, remembering the day the lights came on and I realized what I'd gotten myself into. "I made copies of everything; I returned all the originals Carlos had given me and avoided him like the plague, but he tracked me down. It turned out Carlos was part of some Mexican syndicate. The last time I saw him, I told him I'd given copies of everything he'd ever given me to a lawyer and they would be sent to the police along with his name and a list of everyone I'd ever seen him with if anything happened to me." I could feel myself shivering at the memory. "Of course I didn't, but he had no idea, and a few weeks later I got the call from Grandpa and figured a change of scenery would be a good thing."

"Do you think you were followed?" John asked, peering around the room.

"No. Carlos was never particularly subtle. He was gorgeous, among other things, but never particularly smart. When I left San Francisco, I sent everything I had anonymously to the FBI. I really wanted to just disappear and never see him again so I could try to forget what an idiot I was. I didn't do anything for him, and most of what he gave me to work on was way above my abilities, but Carlos figured one computer geek was as good as another. What he gave me was pretty incriminating, and he's in federal prison the last I heard. Still, getting out of California was probably a good thing, and I like it here. I can work anywhere, and now I have you and Bryce to work with." I smiled, wondering if John thought I was a complete idiot. I'd definitely felt like one at the time. "I certainly should have known that a guy like Carlos wanted something from me," I mumbled, and John tightened his hold on my hand.

"I don't know about that. You're a handsome man, and anyone would be lucky to know you," John told me, and I stared at him for a few seconds, wondering if he was sincere. And he certainly appeared to be, especially as he moved his face closer to mine. John slid his hand up my arm and shoulder, cupping my head as he brought us into a kiss. During our previous kiss, I'd taken charge, but this time I held back, even though my instinct was to surge forward. John quickly deepened the kiss, alternately tugging on my lips and thrusting his tongue deep into my mouth.

I whimpered like a child, wanting more while at the same time wanting John to give it to me, instead of me just taking. And he did. It almost seemed like John could read my mind, but maybe he was reading my body. I'd been told once that my body language was always a giveaway to what I was feeling. John seemed to be picking up on that, kissing hard and then gentling exactly when I needed him to.

We both came up for air with a gasp. I saw John stand up and slowly glide around the counter, sliding his hands along my leg as he approached. Without thinking, I parted my legs and John stepped between them. I was about to stand up as well, but John kept me on the stool as he pressed close and kissed me again. This time there was no counter between us and no way to hide my excitement. My legs bounced and my arms shook as John stroked his tongue along my teeth before plunging in once again, sucking and licking with a force that made my head throb. "John," I gasped when he pulled back slightly. "We need to stop or…."

"Or what?" John challenged, flicking his tongue with feather lightness along my upper lip.

"I won't be able to stop," I croaked, closing my eyes. Somehow I needed to lessen the near sensory overload that threatened to rush over me and wash away the very last of my tenuous hold on any kind of restraint. "We need to take this kind of slow," I muttered almost under my breath, half hoping John wouldn't hear and I'd have an excuse to explore the warm skin and body I'd been watching and imagining for weeks.

John stopped and moved away, both of us breathing hard. I knew I was flushed, and I could feel the blood coursing through me, most of it still pooled in my groin. "You're probably right," John said reluctantly, and I slipped off the stool onto wobbly legs and waited for my mind to clear. "I think I should be going."

I didn't want him to leave. "I was going to find something for dinner…." I knew it was a backhanded invitation, but I didn't want him to feel pressured. What I got was a smile and another kiss that left me panting for more and ready to suggest we skip dinner and go upstairs for dessert. But I restrained myself and enjoyed the sweet kiss. "I think we'd better go eat."

"I'll follow you," John said, and after I grabbed my wallet and keys, we headed out. I'd like to say we found a little quiet, romantic place for dinner, but instead we ended up at a chain steakhouse on the commercial strip. The food was good, even if the restaurant was a bit noisy and filled with tourists, but in the end it didn't seem to matter, because we talked and told each other our silliest jokes, which we both laughed at, and then we talked some more. It really felt like a date but without the usual nerves and queasy stomach. When the server brought the check, I paid, and then we walked out into the evening heat. The air assaulted us as we walked across the parking lot. At our cars, we stopped and stared at each other for a few seconds before laughing nervously. I wanted to kiss him good-bye, but there were things you didn't do in a South Dakota parking lot, and that was definitely one of them. Clapping John on the shoulder, I moved toward my car. "I'll see you after you get back from seeing the ugly white woman." I smiled as I used John's name for her, and he nodded nervously before opening his car door and getting inside. I did the same, then pulled out of the parking lot and drove home.

I thought about going to work but decided against it. I ignored the television for a while but kept thinking about John. After turning it off, I wandered through the empty house for a while before deciding to clean up and go to bed. I'd spent months here alone, but after a few kisses and dinners, things had changed. It was nice having someone to spend time with besides the occasional evenings with Peter and Leonard.

In the bathroom upstairs, I stripped out of my clothes and threw them in the hamper, reminding myself that I desperately needed to do laundry or going to work in my underwear was going to be my only option. Closing the hamper lid, I started the water and then stepped under the warmth. As usual, I washed my hair and then myself, having every intention of making this quick so I could get to bed, but my imagination definitely had ideas of its own. My eyes drifted closed, and I saw John's figure through the patterned shower door and then the glass slid aside and there he was in all his red bronze glory. He stepped into the shower, and then his hands were on my skin, a palm against my chest, his fingers teasing around a nipple. I began to shake and my breath caught. I could almost see John lowering himself onto his knees, the water pouring over us. When the heat of his mouth surrounded me, the water cooled by comparison to the molten, wet heat of his mouth. I thrust my hips, and John met each movement, the suction and tightness overpowering, and then I couldn't contain myself any longer, coming in a rush, crying out, the sound echoing off the tile.

I gasped for breath as water poured onto me, cooling rapidly. I blinked a few times before reaching over to turn off the cool water, trying to throw off the last of my delusion. My skin still tingled from John's imaginary touch as I stepped out of the shower and dried myself with a towel. Still wishing the real John were with me, I cleaned up the room and pulled back the covers of my bed.

Resting on my back, staring up at the ceiling, I imagined what it would be like to have John lying beside me. I couldn't help wondering if this fascination with John was like all the previous times. When I'd first seen Carlos, with his olive skin, chiseled face, the body out of a dream, I'd felt much the same way. When we weren't together, I wished we were and kept imagining what he'd be like. Of course, I know now that the best times I had with Carlos were in my own imagination, because the actual Carlos rarely measured up. As I watched the light of the occasional passing car play on the ceiling, I wondered if that was what I was doing with John. I'd done it so many times, not just with Carlos, although he was the worst. I'd felt the same way with all my previous boyfriends, and I wondered if…. Sighing, I rolled onto my side and closed my eyes. I didn't want what I felt for John to be merely what I'd felt for Carlos. I wanted it to be real, and I hoped it was. "I'm a fool," I said out loud to the empty room. At least I'd forced myself to take my time, and that was the only thing that would tell me if what I was hoping for with John was real or just my imagination.

CHAPTER
# FIVE

I WAS at work when Bryce came in the following morning. I hadn't slept much, and my head hurt. I'd taken something and was sitting at my desk, trying to concentrate. "Where's John?" Bryce asked, and I looked up from the screen, my head grateful for the break.

"He had an appointment and is going to be late." It wasn't my place to tell Bryce John's business. "He'll be in a bit later." I settled back behind my computer but found it difficult to concentrate. "Give me a quick rundown on what you're working on. Are you having any issues?" I stood up and moved toward the small table I'd added to the office. It gave us a place to eat lunch as well as someplace away from our desks where we could lay things out and talk.

"Let me get my stuff," Bryce answered excitedly, and I sat down while he hurried to his desk before returning with his latest updates. "I've got everything done and ready for the integration next week, and I'm working on the next set of projects you gave me," Bryce told me proudly, handing me his check sheets. "I've tested them twice. I believe John is almost done too, and I'm hoping when he comes in, we can check each other's applications before sending them to you."

"You went over all the specifications?" I asked, and Bryce nodded with a grin.

"I also looked up the original requirements that you wrote up and verified against those too, and I found a discrepancy I wanted to ask you about." Bryce pulled out the document, and we reviewed it. I supplied that what he'd found was a change agreed on with the customer, but it was a good catch nonetheless, and I was proud of him for pointing it out. It meant he was looking, and that was good. We went through everything he had so far.

"It looks like I'm the holdup," I commented, knowing I had the most difficult parts of the system. "We'll be ready by next week," I added with a smile. "We're in better shape than I expected."

Bryce stood up and walked quietly back to his desk, the humming of the air conditioner the only real sound in the room. There was something a bit off, and I wondered what it was. "Can I ask a question?" Bryce inquired.

I swallowed when I saw Bryce turn around. "Is there something going on between you and John?" Bryce stepped cautiously back to the table. "I see the way he looks at you sometimes, especially yesterday, and I know you watch him. At first I thought it was because you wanted to keep an eye on him for some reason, but now I think you like each other."

"I guess we do," I confessed. "Nothing has really happened between us, but I do like him." I looked up from the table. "But no matter what, all business will be conducted professionally, and I won't favor him over you if something comes of this." I had no idea if anything would, even though I was hopeful—very hopeful after last night. "We're taking things sort of slow and... this is a little difficult to talk about."

To my surprise, Bryce chuckled slightly before sitting down across from me. "You're a fair man, Jerry, and you're also a pretty lonely one. I don't begrudge you this, as long as you can be happy." Bryce smiled his whitest smile. "Just before you hired me, I met Percy." Bryce giggled and covered his mouth with his hand. "I can't get over that name," Bryce said with another giggle. "Why his mom would name him that, I don't know, but she did, and he's really sweet to me."

"Is that why you're always in a hurry to leave?" I asked, and Bryce blushed slightly.

"Percy works weird hours as a nurse, so I usually get to see him only at dinnertime, and then he has to go to work," Bryce explained.

"If you want to come in and leave an hour earlier, that's fine. As long as you get your work done properly, I wouldn't have a problem with that." I usually started an hour before they got here anyway, so it wouldn't make a difference to me, but I could see where it would be great for Bryce.

I saw him grin. "Really?" You'd think I'd given him a special gift.

"Sure. Now, I think we both have some work to do," I said as I stood up and turned toward my desk. "I'd like to meet Percy sometime." He sounded nice, and I was curious about the kind of guy that would capture Bryce's attention. Bryce promised that he'd bring him by, and returned to his desk. By the time I reached my desk, the main sound I heard over the air conditioner was Bryce's furious typing.

My headache finally gone, I went to work, but found I kept one eye on the door, looking for John. I began to get worried as the morning wore on, and then I finally heard the sound of footsteps outside, and the door opened as John came in. He went directly to his desk, and I heard him moving around, along with whispering between him and Bryce. Peering around my monitor,

74

I tried to catch his eye, but John was either preoccupied or avoiding me. "Fuck," I growled under my breath. I'd been pretty free with my advice to John, and what if he'd taken it and I'd helped make things worse for him? I kept looking around my monitor, but John stayed behind his.

At lunchtime, I brought things from the house, and we ate at the table, with John avoiding talking to either Bryce or me. Once he'd finished eating, Bryce gave me an understanding look and then left the office, saying he was going to take a brief walk in the sunshine. "What happened, John?" I asked once the door closed behind Bryce.

"She… she told me I haven't had my job long enough." John looked up at me. He appeared near tears. "Every time I do what she wants, she tells me I have to do something else." I heard a break in his voice.

"Can you visit them?" I asked, and John nodded slowly.

"She said no at first, and then I did what you said and told her I wanted to speak to her supervisor to see what he said, and she relented. I can visit them on Saturday for a few hours."

John appeared nervous and upset. "I do what she wants, but it's never enough," John said, sounding defeated. "I'm never going to be able to get them."

"Yes, you are. You're doing very well, and I'll write you a letter each week if I have to," I told him gently. This woman was really starting to piss me off, and I'd never met her. I understood following the rules and processes, but changing the rules all the time wasn't fair. "The kids are outside Chamberlain, aren't they?" I asked, and John nodded.

"I'm going to need to rent a car, because the one I have isn't reliable enough to get me there and back," John commented, and I could almost see him making a list in his mind of things he was going to need to do.

"If you like, I'll take you," I offered.

"I can't ask you to do that," John said.

"You didn't—I offered," I countered with a smile. "I know it isn't the answer you were hoping for," I added, touching John's hand. "But you'll get to see them, and that's a step forward." I tried to be encouraging. "You won a battle today with the ugly white woman, and once you've seen the kids and they see you, I know you'll feel better." John stared at his feet, and I took a chance. "You need to be strong for them, because if you give up, then Mato and Ichante have no hope of ever having a home." John lifted his head, and his gaze locked onto mine, its intensity startling in its anger.

"I need to remember who I am and what my name means," he said firmly. "I'll win this war one battle at a time." John's posture straightened and his eyes blazed. In an instant, I could see John's heritage flame inside him. With his back straight and head high, John walked to his desk and sat down, saying nothing. Bryce returned and went back to work as well. They didn't talk back and forth the way they usually did. Glancing around my monitor a few times, I caught Bryce looking back once. He shrugged and went back to work.

After nearly an hour, it was John who broke the silence. "Jerry," he said, and I looked around my monitor, "I appreciate your offer, and I'd like you to go with me on Saturday."

"No problem," I answered, and we shared a brief smile before returning to work. After that, I heard Bryce whisper a question, and then the two of them moved to the table, spending some time talking about the applications they were working on in whispered voices like they usually did. I returned to my work, smiling to beat the band. When I'd offered to take John to visit his niece and nephew, I had figured he'd turn me down because he wanted to go alone. We hadn't known each other that long, and I wasn't sure he'd trust me enough to go. I knew this trip was going to leave John vulnerable, and so did he. It took trust to let someone else see you when you were vulnerable, and it was that trust that made me smile.

SATURDAY morning I got up early. John had said that he was expected at ten thirty in Chamberlain, and with the directions he'd been given, John wanted extra time to make sure he could find the place. It was just after eight, and I was already showered, dressed, and having my first cup of coffee. I figured if we were on the road by eight thirty, we'd be in really good shape. I kept listening for John and finally heard him pull into the driveway. I stepped out onto the porch and saw him looking nervous as he joined me. "I think we better get going," I said, and John nodded stiffly. I finished my coffee and grabbed a cooler I'd packed before heading out of the house.

John met me near the car with a bag, and we loaded the things into the back seat and settled in for a largely uninteresting drive. The freeway in this part of the state crossed land that was largely flat, dotted by the occasional farm or ranch, and every now and then a town of some sort would break up the landscape, but otherwise there wasn't much to look at. "I appreciate you going with me," John said as he stared out the window.

I reached across the seat and touched his hand. "I'm happy to help."

"I brought the toys like you suggested. They had to be sent from the reservation, and they just arrived yesterday," John said, continuing to stare at the passing land.

"John, why aren't your parents trying to get custody?" I'd always wondered.

"My mother tried, but she still has my youngest brother and sister at home." John shuddered. "I think Mom was afraid to because if she applied in earnest, then social services would investigate her, and my youngest sister is only twelve." John left the rest unsaid, and I shivered. These people seemed more like family terrorists than social services.

"I'd have thought the goal would be to keep families together as much as possible," I said as a shiver went down my spine.

"So would I, but there's a lot of money involved. The way things are set up, the money the state gets to take care of children gets allocated to social services and not to the general state treasury, so they have an incentive to keep the money coming in," John said, and I glanced over in time to see his scowl.

"I know you've been in the middle of this for a while, but how did you find all this out?" I asked.

"I had a sociology professor who'd studied all this, and he covered it in class. At the time, the students were outraged, and there was even talk of a letter-writing campaign, but nothing really came of it except that I learned a great deal about why I was being fought at every step." John's voice was rough and hard. "It sucks that people let money stand in the way of families, but that's what's happening, and my niece and nephew are trapped in the middle of it!" His frustration and venom surprised me at first, but I figured John was allowed.

"How did the state get to the kids?" I asked.

"The state has limited power on the reservations, but my sister was living in Mitchell when she died, and social services stepped in before any of us could get there. The kids needed to be taken care of, and the state got involved. Foster care is meant to be temporary, and once I arrived, I expected to be given custody. Boy, was I wrong. I was met with a wall of paperwork, forms, and questions, all designed to keep Native American children in the hands of the state." John was very earnest, and I heard him shift in the seat. "I know it sounds like I'm overreacting, and initially I doubted it myself, but the more I deal with them, the more I'm starting to think South Dakota is part of communist Eastern Europe rather than the United States, with the amount of power they wield over people's lives." John shifted back in his seat, once again staring out the window. "If I ever do get custody of the kids, I'm seriously thinking of moving out of state so they can't take them again."

Without thinking, I gripped the steering wheel more tightly at the thought of John leaving, but I kept myself from saying anything. I knew that if John got custody of his niece and nephew, they would need to be the most important people in his life.

We drove in silence for a while, and John finally settled back in the seat. "I remember the first time I saw that when I was a kid," John commented in reference to a sign for the Mitchell Corn Palace. "My dad took us to visit some friends in Minnesota, and he stopped there on the way so we could run around for a while. I thought it was so cool."

"I did too. The last time I drove west, I stopped. As a kid, I thought it was fascinating, and I remember standing outside looking up at the murals, but as an adult, it seemed to have lost some of its luster. It's still interesting, but maybe in a sort of tacky, tourist-trappy sort of way."

John nodded slowly. "I have to agree, but it's still pretty neat, and if I get the kids, I'm going to take them there so they can see it."

"When you get the kids, you can take them to see all kinds of things," I added, and John smiled a thank-you sort of smile.

We traveled for the better part of another hour before pulling up in front of a small but neat house in Chamberlain. "This is it," John said softly, making no effort to get out right away, and I heard him sigh. "It looks nice." The hedges were neatly clipped, and the yard appeared immaculately kept. A few toys could be seen on the walk, but that was the only thing that broke up the white-picket-fence perfection. John opened his door.

"I'll hang back and let you greet them alone," I said as I opened my door. As John reached for the toys he'd brought, I took the bag so he'd have his hands free. As we crossed the street, I saw the front door of the house open. A little boy stepped out, followed by an older girl. Once John got across the street, the girl raced across the lawn. "Uncle Akecheta!" she cried, and she launched herself into John's arms. Mato followed behind, running as fast as his little legs could carry him, and John folded him into his arms too. I stood back and watched John. I saw tears in his eyes as he hugged both of them. I couldn't understand what he was saying, but that didn't matter, the cries and hugs from all of them saying more than words could ever express.

"I thought you forgot us," Ichante said once she'd stepped back.

"Never," John said, his voice nearly breaking, and then he hugged her again before falling on his butt on the grass. Both kids tried to climb onto his lap at the same time, practically crawling over each other to get to him.

"Can we go home with you?" Ichante asked.

"Not now, but hopefully very soon," John answered, and a lump formed in my throat, knowing how much it must be tearing at John to have to give that answer. "Let me look at you," John said, and Ichante stepped back and twirled like a ballerina. I saw John reach out and touch her head, running his hand through her short hair and then pulling Ichante back into another hug. Mato clung to John, and while I was sure John was speaking to him, Mato refused to let go and simply nodded his answers.

A slight woman appeared in the open doorway, wiping her hands on her apron. "Ione, Mike, bring your uncle inside," she called lightly. John stood up, bringing Mato with him, holding Ichante's hand as he walked toward the front door.

THE GOOD FIGHT

"This is Jerry. He's my…." John hesitated for a split second, then said, "… friend."

"Jerry Lincoln, ma'am," I said, and I extended my hand.

"Mary Caruthers," she said before taking it lightly in hers for a quick handshake. "I'm glad John is able to see the children. They ask about him all the time." I did a double-take before turning to John and then looking back at Mrs. Caruthers. Something wasn't right, and I couldn't quite put my finger on it. "Please have a seat in the living room," she offered with a sweep of her arm. "I'll get some refreshments," Mary said a little nervously before hurrying away.

John sat on the sofa with a kid on either side of him, talking excitedly. Mary returned and placed a tray with a pitcher of what looked like lemonade, plastic glasses, and a sippy cup on the coffee table. Mary poured glasses for us before handing the sippy cup to Mato.

The house appeared immaculately clean, and as I looked, I saw that both kids appeared to be well cared for. I was afraid they would be living in poor conditions. At least that wasn't a worry.

"Who is he?" Mato asked, pointing at me after he'd sipped for a while.

"That's Mr. Jerry, and he's a friend of mine," John said, looking at me, and I smiled my encouragement. "He and I work together."

"What do you do?" Mary asked as she sat on the edge of one of the chairs, looking at me.

"I'm a computer programming consultant. I develop websites and complex web-based applications." I knew I was probably speaking over her head a little, but I wanted her to be impressed. "I've been working with John for a few weeks, and he's quite talented." I also figured that since I was here as a friend

81

and not John's boss, that I'd play it cool. Mary smiled, and I looked back over at John.

"I brought something for you," John said, which was my cue to hand him the bag I was still carrying. John reached inside and pulled out a small bundle wrapped in a bit of cloth. "A friend of mine made it for you, and a friend of your mother's wove the cloth for you." Mato took the bundle in his little hands, turning it over a few times. The cloth fell away and Mato held up a carved wooden horse. "Someday you'll be able to ride a horse like that," John said, and Mato wriggled off his lap and began playing on the floor. Mary stepped over and picked up the cloth, and I saw her run it through her fingers.

"I'll make sure this is put with his things," Mary said. "Is it a traditional pattern?"

"Yes," John answered in a strained voice. Then he reached into the bag and pulled out another bundle in a nearly identical piece of cloth, handing it to Ichante. She took it warily and slowly unwrapped it. I had never seen children move so intently when it came to presents, and I saw her look at Mary, who nodded slightly. As soon as the cloth fell away and she saw the simple doll, Ichante squealed her delight and began saying things in what I assumed was the Lakota language. Whatever was being said, it was obvious that the doll was a huge hit, not only from the words, but from the way she alternately clutched it to herself and then held it so she could stroke the red-brown face.

"Would it be okay if we took the children to lunch?" I asked Mary, and she seemed a bit nervous. "We'll understand if you wish to come along." I had no idea what social services had told her, and I didn't want to cause trouble. I just wanted to give John as much time with the kids as possible.

Mary seemed to think about it for a long time. "There's a diner in town, and we could meet you there," she finally said.

"Thank you," John said as Mato climbed back onto the sofa and into John's lap, showing him the horse as he pattered on. I wasn't sure if he was speaking English or Lakota, because I could hardly understand him, but John seemed to understand every word. Picking up my glass, I poured some more lemonade and sipped it while John played with the children. Every now and then he would look up to me with an almost heartbroken expression on his face and then go back to the kids. Other than the fact that he was going to have to leave eventually, I had no idea why he was so hurt. I wanted to tell him to make the most of the time he had, but kept quiet and let him play.

After a while, Mato slid down onto the floor, still holding his horse, and then raced down the hall. "Walk, please," Mary said, and Mato slowed down. He returned a few minutes later carrying the horse John had given him in one hand and a plastic horse in the other. Then he galloped them over the sofa cushions and around John's legs. Ichante sat on the edge of the sofa, cradling and talking to her doll as she combed its long black hair with her fingers.

From the outside, the scene looked incredibly loving and tranquil, with John playing with the kids, but I knew that just below the surface sadness and pain lurked for both John and the kids, because eventually we'd have to leave. Mato continued playing and crawling all over John with fits and giggles. "He rarely sounds like that," Mary said, turning to me. "The children miss their mother, and they ask about their uncle all the time." Again her expression showed confusion, and I looked back toward John. We definitely needed to talk as soon as we were alone.

"I'm hungry," Ichante said, moving closer to John.

"We're going to have lunch with your uncle, so go wash your hands, and we'll get into the car." Mary stood up, and John did as well.

"I'll help them," he said, and Mary told him where the bathroom was. John took each of the kids by the hand, and they led him to the bathroom. I knew from the expression that flashed for a brief second that John was determined to spend every moment he could with them.

Once they were done, John brought the children back, and Mary gave us directions to the diner. "It's on the main street of town, just two blocks away. We'll meet you there in a few minutes," she said as she walked us to the door. We left, and I followed John through the intense heat and sun to the car. The inside of the car was boiling, and I held the door open to let the heat out before starting the engine and cranking up the air conditioner. John remained quiet for the short ride, and I found the restaurant and parked out front. We headed inside and found a table large enough for all of us. I sat down, but John seemed jumpy and he went back outside.

He rejoined me with Mato in his arms and Ichante holding his hand. Mary followed, and I made room for her at the table while John and the kids sat together on the other side. They chattered about what they wanted to eat, and John let them order what they wanted. The server stopped by, and Mary helped with the drink orders. She seemed firm, but very patient. John's attention was on the kids as he helped them color their placemats.

"Your work must be challenging," Mary commented as she sipped her water. "Are you from here?"

"I grew up just outside Sioux Falls. I learned all about computers while I was in California." We chatted, making small talk, and I told her about returning to take care of my grandfather. The entire time she paid attention but had one eye on the kids in what I thought was a rather motherly, caring way. The server returned with the drinks, and we ordered the food while the kids barely looked up from their coloring. By the time it arrived, the server brought fresh placemats for the kids, and they ate and chattered about this and that. Whatever the kids needed, John was there to help them.

As the meal continued, I could see the tension slowly slip into John's body. He knew the time was coming when he'd have to say good-bye. By the time everyone was done eating, John's body was strung so tight I thought he was going to begin playing music. Both kids presented Uncle Akecheta with their drawings, and he hugged each of them tightly. Mato climbed onto his lap, holding his uncle, his face buried in John's neck.

"Will you come back to see us?" Ichante asked once they were out on the sidewalk. John knelt down and placed Mato back onto his feet.

"I'll be back to see both of you as soon as I can. I promise," he said, and I could hear the heartbreak in his voice. I had to turn away briefly to wipe my eyes. John gave each of the kids another hug, and then Mary said good-bye and bundled the kids into a minivan. John stood on the sidewalk and waved until they'd pulled away and the van was out of sight. Then he moved toward the car and got in the passenger seat once I unlocked the doors.

I started the car, and we headed out toward the freeway. John said nothing, once again staring out the window, suppressed rage washing off him. I kept quiet, hoping that John would talk when he was ready, so we rode in silence until we saw the first sign for the Corn Palace.

"Those kids know nothing about their heritage. Ichante can remember only a little Lakota, and Mato knows almost none at all." John faced the window as he spoke. "And she keeps cutting their hair!" John practically wailed. "It was cut after their mother died, but it should be allowed to grow again until someone else close to them dies." John banged his fist on the dashboard, and I jumped, the car swerving.

"Do you know what Mato told me when he brought out his toy horse?" John's rage was barely under control. "He said he plays cowboys and Indians, and he makes Ichante be the Indian so he can shoot her." John began pounding his leg, and I pulled the car off to the side of the road. "That woman is killing my family with her lemonade and oppression." I stopped the car, and John got out, walking toward the side of the road. I stayed back and let him have some time to himself. For a few seconds, he paced back and forth along the side of the freeway like some sort of caged cat looking for a way out. Then without warning, he lifted his head and let loose a cry so filled with anguish I felt it searing its way down my spine.

I got back in the car, settled in my seat, and waited for John. He continued prowling in the afternoon heat for a while, and then I heard the passenger door open, and he slid back into the seat and fastened his seat belt. Then I pulled back onto the freeway and gave him time with his thoughts. "That woman," John swore, "is stealing their heritage and trying to keep me away."

"John, I don't think she's your enemy," I said slowly, and if looks could kill, I'd have been dead and burned to ashes.

"How can you say that?" John asked between clenched teeth, his anger once again rising to the surface. "She's bulldozing away any sense of their heritage they might have had. Ichante's room has Barbie, and Mato has a room with Star Wars posters. Other than what I gave them, they have nothing of their heritage and no way to learn about it."

"I understand," I said calmly.

"Do you?" he shot back. "Because I don't see how you possibly could." The venom was cutting.

"I'm not your enemy either," I said levelly, trying to keep from lashing out. I took a few deep breaths before continuing, because my instinct was to reach over the seat and slap him on the back of the head to knock some sense into him. "If she was your enemy and trying to keep you away from the kids, then why did she tell me that the kids miss you and ask why you hadn't visited? Because she did, while you were playing with the kids. Who was it that kept you from seeing them? Mary may not know anything about your heritage, but she's caring for those kids as best she can, and I'll wager she's going to miss them very much once they're gone. Like I said, I don't think she's your enemy." I continued driving and waited for John to speak again.

It took quite a while, but when he did, he sounded much calmer. "Did she really say that?"

"Yes. I got the distinct feeling she couldn't understand why you hadn't visited them all these months, and if she was wary and cautious, it was because you'd stayed away. So if you can let go of your anger and start thinking clearly, then maybe we can figure out how to fight the real enemy."

"The ugly white woman," John said.

"Exactly. The ugly white woman," I echoed, and John gave me a slight smile as some of his anger slipped away.

"So what do we do?" John asked after a while.

"Not sure, but there's strength in numbers. So we need to get as many supporters as we possibly can. I think you need to contact as many people as you can—tribe members and white people. See if you can get them to write letters of support. The next time you see the ugly white woman, you need to show her you aren't alone."

"What will that do?" John asked skeptically.

"It'll let her know that you have friends who care, because if those friends will write letters for you, they'll also write to legislators and government officials. Bureaucrats will only step out of their comfortable little boxes if you force them to. The ugly white woman"—God, I really needed to know her name because that sounded stupid coming from me—"needs a push to get her to do what she should. So we'll push hard."

"We? You'll help?" John asked, and I nodded.

"If I can. You need to get letters of support from people who've known you for a while. I suggest asking some of your professors, especially ones that had you for more than one class. They should be willing to write a letter of support. You could also ask your past employers," I suggested, and I could see that John wasn't convinced, but I didn't have any other ideas, beyond waiting months until John had been working longer.

"I'll give it a try," John agreed as I took the exit. We made our way through the city to the house, and I parked in the driveway next to John's car.

"Would you like to come in for a while?" It was still late afternoon, and I figured something to drink would go down pretty well. After standing, I grabbed the cooler and carried it into the house. "What can I get for you?"

John shook his head and moved closer. "I'm sorry, Jerry. I shouldn't have taken my anger and frustration out on you." He moved still closer, and I wanted to pull him into a hug but held back. "You have done nothing but try to help, and I know you care and that you're on my side."

"I am," I said softly, and I wondered just what John was going to do now. I stepped back slightly, and my back touched the counter. John stepped closer once again.

"I shouldn't have taken my anger out on you," John said as heat radiated off his body.

"You have every right to be upset, but be upset at the right people. Mary Caruthers isn't the enemy, and she could be an ally. She cares for those kids, and she wants them with their family." John lifted his eyebrows. "Don't give me that. She only wants what's best for them, and if you get to know her a little, she may be able to help convince social services that you're able to care for them."

"So what are you saying?" John asked, folding his arms across his chest.

I reached into my pocket. "She gave me her phone number and told me that you could call every few days. The kids would love to talk to you, and she also said that if you called before coming, you'd be free to visit the kids." John's mouth fell open, and he began to shake. Almost before I knew it, John had his arms around me and he'd lifted me off my feet, jumping up and down, shouting and laughing. "John, put me down," I said through my own laughter, and he did. John also kissed me hard, so hard I forgot about everyone and everything except John's lips on mine. Holy fuck, the man could kiss, and I put my arms around his neck, returning the kiss with everything I had. He tasted good and felt even better.

We moved through the house, with John directing me using his lips. The back of my legs hit the edge of the sofa, and I fell backward, with John kissing me all the way down. "You're amazing," John told me after pulling away so we could breathe.

"Is all that for the phone number?" I asked, and John looked deeply into my eyes for a few seconds before kissing me again. No, that was definitely for something much more than the phone number. John shifted, still kissing me, and I felt him kneel on the sofa cushions, pressing me back onto the sofa. I held onto John as he kissed me harder, his weight sandwiching me between the cushions and him, and what a place to be.

"You taste like sunshine," John said, and I chuckled.

"I always thought you smelled like the wind," I told John, inhaling deeply before burying my face in his neck, licking the skin as I floated on his dizzying aroma.

John's intensely energetic kisses continued as zings and sparks shot all through me. My body seemed ready to burst into flame. I tightened my hold on him, afraid he was going to stop but not wanting to say so for fear the kisses would end and I'd be left alone once again. I felt John slide his hand under my shirt, working it up my chest until one of his thumbs plucked and teased a nipple. I made some strangled sound that John swallowed and continued kissing all the way through.

"Jesus!" I cried between gasps for air when John lifted his lips from mine. Both talking and thinking were now difficult activities, and all I wanted was to disappear into John's deep, dark eyes. "Don't you dare stop!"

"I have no intention of stopping until you're mine!" John growled and then captured my mouth. John's touch never stilled, and as we kissed, I felt the warmth of his rough fingers along my side and up my chest. I could barely move with John's delicious weight on top of me, but my back arched on its own when John plucked my nipples hard, swirling and caressing the sensitive flesh until I thought my head would explode. "Lift your arms," John whispered, and I forced them away from his skin. John shifted my shirt up further and along my arms until it crumpled to the floor. I had no time to wonder about it as John caressed my arms, making them tingle and twitch. My shoulders were next, and John lifted his body as his caresses traveled down my chest and to my stomach. By the time I realized what was happening, John was kneeling by my legs, and I peered up at him through half-closed eyes, half under his spell, wondering where he'd gone.

"Upstairs?" I asked between short, shallow breaths, and John stood up, offering his hand. I took it, and he helped me to my feet before heading toward the stairs. At the top, I took the lead and led John to my bedroom.

John kissed me once we reached the doorway, and I felt him press me back against the bed. We fell in a tumbled tangle of arms and legs. Our kiss broke long enough for John to struggle out of his shirt, and as his chest stretched over me, I clamped my lips around a dark nipple, sucking and getting my first real taste of his body. He tasted earthy and rich, and I wanted it all, everything all at once. I let my hands roam over every bit of skin within touching distance as he struggled with his T-shirt. I suppose I was making it difficult for him to concentrate, but I didn't care. John's chest hovered over my lips, and I couldn't resist licking and kissing every bit of skin within lip distance.

I heard John sigh and felt his body shift as he moved away. He pressed his chest to mine, and I couldn't suppress a sigh. John's skin felt heavenly against mine, smooth and hot. Our mouths met in a fierce kiss that quickly turned into a battle for dominance that I let him win. John needed to feel in control right now, and I wanted to accept whatever he was willing to give. John's lips nibbled and sucked on mine, his teeth lightly scraping over sensitive skin. John shifted slightly above me as I felt him work open my belt. The buckle clanged slightly, and then the leather parted, followed by the catch of my jeans. John teased the skin at the top of my jeans and then he pressed his hands beneath me and into my pants, palms and fingers cupping my butt, kneading the flesh. "Damn, you feel hot," John mumbled between kisses, and I felt him grip me, tight and hard, fingers digging in, and I loved it.

I'd always liked men who understood that I wasn't going to break. Not that I liked being hit or anything, but I liked being touched by someone who knew that more was definitely better. John understood that. His calloused fingers added just that sense of roughness that threatened to send me over the edge.

Then John's touch gentled and moved away. I lifted my head and watched as he stepped away from the bed, watching me. For a second I felt exposed. Then John smiled—no, not a smile, but some intensely erotic combination of a lustful leer and a pleased grin that sent a shot of passion straight to my throbbing cock. Leaning forward, John flipped off my shoes and then grabbed my jeans and roughly tugged them off my legs, dumping the jeans onto the floor. The rest of my clothes followed, and I lay naked and exposed under his intense gaze.

"Don't move," he said in a gravelly whisper, and I heard his shoes thunk on the floor. Then I watched as John's long fingers opened his belt and then parted the fabric of his pants. The denim slid down his legs. When he stood up again I noticed two things—his hair had fallen over his face, and he flipped it aside as my gaze shifted to the other fact, that John was completely and totally naked... in my bedroom... with me.

To say his hairless body was magnificent would be the understatement of the century. Rich skin the color of the earth shimmered and stretched over work-hardened muscle as he slowly prowled toward me. I wanted to sit up and reach for him, but I couldn't move a muscle. He had me completely enthralled, and with each step, his heavy, full cock swayed slowly from side to side. I gasped, swallowed, and then licked my suddenly dry lips, blinking a few times to make sure I wasn't dreaming. "Imagined you many times," I mumbled with near incoherence. "Never came close to reality."

I was mesmerized by every movement of John's body—his thick legs as he climbed onto the bed, his strong arms as he reached for me, his rough hands that held me down, and his firm, soft lips that devoured my own. John's weight pressed me into the mattress, his skin sliding against mine, a body so smooth, it almost felt as though he'd been oiled. His cock rested against my throbbing hard dick, every touch making it jump between us.

John pulled his lips from mine as he slid down my body, his hips, stomach, and then chest running along my length. I bit my lip trying to stifle a groan that burst from deep in my chest. John kissed long trails over my skin, lapping at my nipples before kissing a trail down my side that had me squirming with near ticklish anticipation. I arched my back and tried to move closer to get that little bit more of sensation that seemed to elude me. "Don't move," John warned, and my eyes widened.

"Is that what you like?" I asked, wondering how I felt about being commanded while in bed.

"To give you pleasure, yes. To keep you on a knife's edge for hours and then push you with just the slightest touch until you fall into the abyss of ecstasy, yes. That is exactly what I like." John's eyes blazed, and while I might have had doubts, my body didn't. It vibrated and throbbed with unbridled anticipation. "Will you let me?" John asked, and I answered yes before I could even think about it. "Then get on your hands and knees."

John moved away, and I rolled over, positioning myself the way he'd said. John ran his hand down my spine, and I shivered. "God...." I groaned softly.

"Lower your head and leave your butt in the air," John told me firmly as he ran his palm over my cheek. Grabbing a pillow, I held it as John caressed my skin. The bed shifted, and John stroked my sides. I felt him press his hips to my butt, and his cock slid between my legs and along my hanging balls. I made no sound; I couldn't, my mouth hanging open in wonder as John kissed a slow line down my neck, along my back. He pulled his hips away as he moved lower, and a string of tingles raced up and down my back again and again, each one intensifying and building on the last until they felt like unending ripples in a pond. The hot, searing wetness continued lower, and I held my breath, my eyes clamping closed as I wished and prayed for John to continue but didn't dare hope he would.

"Jesus God!" I cried as John's tongue blazed a hot trail down my cleft, sliding past my opening and then down to my balls. I felt John's hand encircle my dick, pulling it back as his tongue continued its explorations. My legs shook and rocked on the bed, my fingers clutching the pillow as I gasped and moaned, trying to catch the breath that seemed to have been ripped from me. And just when I was able to catch a deep breath, John nibbled the skin of my opening and then speared me deep and hard with his tongue. I came unglued, crying out, falling forward until I was splayed on the bed. John used my new position to his advantage, spreading me wide and then licking and sucking my butt until I could barely see straight.

I began thrusting, my cock gliding deliciously along the sheets. I started when I felt a light smack across my butt. "Hey!" I protested.

"Then don't move," John growled, and I shivered with excitement. "You're in my hands."

I shook my head and forced my hips to still. John waited, smoothing his hands along my thighs, and then I felt the bed shift and his tongue return to my skin, instantly driving me nearly insane with total wanton desire. I wondered what was next and I didn't have to wait long. My breath caught once again, and I nearly bit my tongue when John slid his hand down my perineum and over my balls before gliding under me and along my shaft. Damn, that felt good, and I willed John to do it again, but he held still, giving me just enough friction to increase my desire. John continued sharpening the knife he'd balanced me on. I had no idea whatsoever how long he'd kept me there. It could have been minutes or hours. I was so far gone.

John flipped me onto my back, and I went willingly. Whatever he wanted, I was ready and willing to give. John raised my ankles, and I brought my knees to my chest, spreading myself in a wantonly hedonistic display. John slid his lips along my length, and just when I thought he was going to tease me, John closed his mouth over my length, taking me deep and hard. For the life of me, I don't know why I didn't come right then. I suppose if I'd been prepared for it, I would have, but it took me a few seconds to get my mind around what was happening to my body, and by then John's lips had slipped away and a finger teased at my entrance. John breached me slowly with a finger. I silently begged him to curl his finger just so, but he didn't. The few times he got close to that spot, I'd gasp, and John would back away. He added a second finger, and the stretch was exquisite.

"Are you about ready for me?" John whispered, and I opened my mouth to answer, but my throat was so dry I couldn't, so I nodded and flopped my head back onto the bed. Swallowing hard, I eventually found my voice.

"God, yes," I finally gasped. My body was wrung out, nearly limp, and I hadn't even come yet. I'd been riding wave crests and troughs for so long I wasn't sure what to expect. I reached over to the nightstand and pulled open the drawer before returning my attention to John.

I watched as he opened a condom and then rolled it down his length. Then John squeezed a dollop of lube onto his fingers. With those digits, he teased my opening before pressing inside, and I groaned, tightening myself around him, wishing I could pull him deeper. Then they slipped out of me, and I whimpered, feeling deprived. I felt John reposition himself between my legs, and then his cock pressed to my entrance and stopped. He throbbed against my skin, and I groaned, trying to move closer, to force John to enter me. His patience was driving me out of my mind, and then, almost in slow motion, John pressed inside.

I felt the head of John's cock breach me and then still. I took deep breaths and waited. After what seemed like forever, he pressed further, slowly entering and filling me. The stretch and burn were rapturous, and I breathed shallow and quick as he continued deeper. My body bloomed around him, taking as much of his thickness as he was willing to give me. I wanted it all, but John had already proven a patient lover, and I knew he'd give me what I wanted in his own time. "How does this feel?" John asked, stopping once again.

"Full, empty," I breathed, "like, more...." God, he actually expected coherent thought at a time like this? Thankfully, he pressed deeper, and I pushed back against him, needing it all right now. I held my breath until John's hips rested against my butt. I scooted down against him, taking John as deep as humanly possible. "Take me!"

John's incredible eyes, as black as night, met mine, and I felt him pull away, his cock rubbing inside me. I came unglued, groaning long and low as he took me halfway to heaven, and once he'd pulled nearly all the way out, he snapped his hips, and I was transported the rest of the way. Over and over again, he did the same thing, driving me almost to the peak and then pulling back, only to do it again. My head rocked and throbbed on the pillow and still he offered me no release. My skin was on fire, my body so filled with tension that I thought I was going to burst into flame at any minute.

The speed of John's movements picked up, and my mind shifted into a different gear. This had to be it. John gripped me hard, stroking me fast and quick. My stomach tightened and I panted. The faster he stroked, the higher I flew. I felt strung so tight, my body filled with so much energy, that as I reached the peak once more, I only hoped I didn't fly apart when John finally allowed my release to wash over me. Gasping, panting, clutching the bedding for dear life, I felt my body reach the peak and then fall into floating nothingness. That lasted two seconds, and then the climax hit me like a runaway freight train. I had no control at all. John's hands and cock had complete control of my body, and all I could do was scream as I rode out the most powerful release of my life. Once it passed, everything around me ceased. I hovered on warm, white, fluffy clouds, my body as light as a feather. I knew the feeling wasn't going to last, but I thought of nothing and willed it to continue.

Opening my eyes, I saw John, unmoving, smiling at me as the world began to spin once again and I became aware of everything around me. Taking a deep breath, I held it and wondered just exactly what had happened to me. "You're fine," John soothed, and I gasped as he slowly pulled out of me. I hadn't even realized he'd come, but John was off the bed and into the bathroom almost before I realized what was happening. My head felt stuffed with cotton, and I let John take care of me.

He returned, wiping me with a warm cloth before drying my skin. When he came back again, I felt the bed dip, and then I was being held tight. "Are you okay?" John whispered into my ear, and I nodded slowly, just to be sure my brains didn't leak out my ears.

"I'm fine. Are you?" I tilted my head and was kissed softly.

"Oh yes. I'm perfect."

"But...." I began, and John shushed me gently, placing a finger over my lips.

"You were amazing, and I may have driven you a little further than I should have," John said, and I wondered what he was talking about, but I still felt kind of floaty, and I was too happy to even think about anything other than simply being. Closing my eyes, I rested my head on John's shoulder as he wrapped his arms around me, and I drifted to sleep.

Waking with a start, I sat up and looked around me. "Carlos," I cried, trying to get away, but when I looked around, he wasn't there. John was sleeping there, naked on the bed, and he stirred long enough to enfold me back into his arms.

"It's okay. He's gone, and I'm here,"' John mumbled, and I settled back on the bed, wondering what the hell had made me think of Carlos all of a sudden. John tugged me to him, spooning against my back as he lightly rubbed my stomach. "Just relax and nap a little while longer," John soothed, and I closed my eyes and tried to relax, but knew there was no way I was going to sleep again. Instead of getting up, though, I listened to the sounds of the house and to John's soft snores. Other than telling John about my ex a while ago, I hadn't thought of Carlos much at all, and I wondered why I was thinking of him now.

# CHAPTER
# SIX

"So," PETER began as he lifted his martini to his lips, "how is every little thing? We haven't seen you in weeks, so there has to be something juicy." Peter winked, and Leonard nudged him with his elbow.

"Leave him alone. If he's happy, and he looks it, then he deserves a bit of privacy, you old busybody," Leonard scolded before looking at me. "You are happy, aren't you?"

"Yes," I answered simply, not holding back my smile.

"So where is he?" Peter asked, making a show of looking around the house.

"We aren't joined at the hip." I used my glass of soda to hide my expression. "He had an appointment, and he said he'd be here once he got done." It was well after five, and I was beginning to wonder if something was wrong. Standing up, I peered outside briefly and then sat back down.

"So what's the occasion?" Peter asked. "You said when you called that you had something to celebrate."

"We turned over a huge project to a customer today. They were pleased and are sending the final payment. That was one of the largest projects I've done to date, and in three weeks we start an even larger one. I'm also beginning to think I'm going to need an office manager. I can't continue to do all the bookkeeping and office organization as well as keep up with the development work I need to do. With these projects, they pay well, but there's a tremendous amount of organization and supporting material that needs to be gathered. I get to bill for that as well as the main body of work, but I just don't have the time."

Peter set down his glass, and I saw him and Leonard share a look that told me something was up. "What is it?" I asked, still listening for the sound of John's car. I was beginning to wonder if he'd gone right home.

"Peter's job is being phased out in a month," Leonard explained bitterly. "They told him today that with business the way it is, the general manager was going to take over his duties and that his services would no longer be required. They're going to pay his severance and vacation, so we should be okay for a while...."

I didn't know what to say. I knew Peter loved that job, and he'd been at the store forever. I also knew they were looking at me like I was their savior. "How are your computer skills?" I asked, and I saw both of them once again look at each other, and the light of hope I'd seen in Peter's eyes faded a little.

"I don't... have them. I used them at the store, but only their systems. I don't have general skills like that." Peter gulped from his glass. "Actually, I was sort of thinking we might be able to help each other. If you don't find someone, I could come work for you and help you with some of your paperwork, if you could help teach me some of the basics about computers so I could get a permanent job." Peter looked worried and frazzled, and I knew I couldn't turn him down. He'd done so much for me.

"How about this—for the next few weeks, starting tomorrow, we've all agreed to work half days on Saturdays to clear up some smaller projects so we can get ready for the really big one. Why don't you come in then, and you can start getting the spreadsheets organized. You can use Excel?" I asked, and Peter nodded. "Good. We'll get you set up, and you can work and learn at the same time."

I heard a car outside and, peering out the window, saw John getting out. I sighed softly when I caught a glimpse of the expression on his face, knowing instantly his meeting with the social worker hadn't gone well. I excused myself and walked to the front door. By the time I opened it, John had a smile on his face that I could tell was a mask. I wanted to ask him what had happened, but refrained as John moved into the living room and greeted Peter and Leonard. After talking for a while, we headed out to dinner. I half expected John to beg off, but he went along, although he remained quiet through most of dinner. He participated in the conversation when pulled in, but otherwise he remained quiet even by his standards.

Once we got back to the house, Peter and Leonard said good night, with Peter saying he'd see me in the morning. Almost as soon as they were gone, the frustration and rage that John had held in burst out in the form of a howl that damned near shook the windows. No one could do that to John faster than the ugly white woman, who I'd learned was actually named Janet Knowles. "What did she do?"

"She said I still need more time on my job. I gave her copies of all the letters, and she actually said she needed the originals," John said between his teeth.

"You didn't give them to her, did you?" I asked quickly, and John glowered at me for a second before his stance softened.

"No. But she made light of everything we've done." John began prowling around the room, pacing like a caged lion. "The kids deserve to be with me. I have a good job, I can take care of them, and I have a place to live with good schools. I'm getting tired of this bitch standing in my way." John stomped hard enough to rattle the floor.

"I wish I had some idea what to do," I said. I was totally stymied, and short of simply waiting her out, I had no idea what else to do. "How about coming for a walk with me? Maybe some fresh air will allow us to think."

"Okay," John agreed, and then he moved closer. "But when we get back, you have to promise to make me forget everything." John nipped at my lips, and I tugged him into a hard kiss. I could certainly do that, especially since making John forget involved him driving me out of my mind.

THE following morning I woke with John next to me. I didn't want to get out of bed and work, especially on a Saturday, but we'd agreed to work, and I knew it was the right thing to do. Looking at the clock, I shook John awake and heard him groan something about leaving him alone. "Bryce and Peter are going to be here in fifteen minutes for work, and unless you want them seeing your bare butt, you need to get dressed." I lightly smacked John's butt, and he groaned again before moving away. Leaning forward, I rubbed his back and then leaned closer. Kissing each of John's nether cheeks, I sucked on the skin.

"What are you doing?" John groaned with a little more vigor.

"Marking your ass as mine," I retorted, and John shifted on the bed. Suddenly I found myself on my stomach, squirming slightly. Then I felt John's lips on my own butt.

"And this is mine." John smoothed his hand over my cheeks, and I moaned softly as he teased the tender flesh around my opening.

"John," I whimpered. "We don't have time." God, I wanted more time. John had taken me to heaven multiple times the night before, and by the time we'd fallen asleep I swear both of us could barely remember our names. John stroked one more time, and then I felt him get up off the bed. Lifting my gaze, I watched his butt as he walked toward the bathroom. Once the door closed, I got up and began pulling on clothes.

John opened the bathroom door and walked naked into the room, stretching toward the ceiling, and I had to keep myself from reaching out to touch, because if I did I'd never get downstairs. Taking my turn in the bathroom, I washed up and shaved before pulling on my shoes and heading downstairs, leaving John to finish dressing.

In the kitchen, I started the coffeepot and opened the doors to the office while waiting for the pot to finish brewing. John came down, and I poured him a mug as I heard a knock on the door. Opening the door, I ushered Peter inside and poured him a mug too. "Let's get to work," I said, and I led the group out to the office. Bryce was already at his desk, and John went to his.

"I'll set you up at the table to start with," I said to Peter, and I went back into the house to retrieve my older laptop. Returning, I saw Peter waiting. After booting up the laptop, I helped Peter open the records I needed to update and provided him with the data that needed to be recorded. "Each of these timesheets needs to be entered into the spreadsheet by customer."

"Okay," Peter said, looking a bit lost.

"Once you have the data entered, I'll show you how to use Excel to help organize and report on it. That should help you get a good understanding of Excel," I told him with a smile, and Peter nodded. Turning to the computer, he began entering the data, and I returned to my desk and got to work.

Unfortunately I didn't get a great deal done, because every time I made progress, Peter needed some sort of help. Halfway through the morning, Bryce finished up a task, so he spent some time with Peter. Finally, by the end of the morning, Peter seemed to be getting what they had been trying to explain, and he settled down to actually work. At noon, I said good-bye to Bryce, who hurried off to spend the afternoon with Percy.

"Is it time to leave?" Peter asked.

"Just about," I answered. "How much more do you have to do?"

"I'm almost done," Peter answered. I looked at John and nodded, and he shut down his computer.

"Then finish up and we'll call it a day." I was anxious to get out of there and spend some time in the fresh air. I shut down my programs and the systems, finishing up as Peter got done as well. I made a note to check his work over later. Leaving everything in the office, we headed into the house.

"Have you had any luck with your niece and nephew?" Peter asked, and John shook his head.

"I appreciate you writing a letter for me, though," John said.

"Of course. Anything I can do to help." They settled around the kitchen table with a fresh pot of coffee. "I was wondering if you've taken your issues to your tribal council. They might be able to help you. Those bodies have some pull in Pierre, and they could help you get heard."

John looked at me, and I nodded. "It can't hurt," I offered.

"I could see when they meet next and see if I can get on their agenda, but they're all the way on the other side of the state, and they meet during the week, so if I go, I'll need some time away," John explained.

"Find out what we need to do, and we'll make whatever arrangements we need to get you heard," I said firmly. "If they can help you get the kids, then I'll close the office for a day and we'll go." I was willing to do whatever was needed to help John get those kids. He had such a big heart, and those two children needed a permanent home. We'd been to visit the kids once more, and we were planning to go the following Saturday afternoon yet again.

"You'd really drive all that way?" John asked as he turned to me.

"Of course I'd take you," I told him with a slight eye roll.

Peter finished his cup of coffee and then stood up. "I need to get home," he said as he placed the empty mug in the sink. He walked toward the door. "I'll see you later."

I waved and said good-bye, and Peter left. John dug into his pocket and pulled out his phone. I listened to half a conversation for a few minutes, most of it in what I assumed was Lakota, as I moved around the room, cleaning up and making lunch. By the time I had sandwiches made, John was hanging up from his call. "How is your mother?" I asked, and John smiled.

"She's good. She said she'll contact the council and get back to me," John replied, and I heard his voice hitch. "She cried over the kids, and then she got angry, so who knows. We may get a call to be there quick because she's known most of the tribal leaders since they were children, and they're all scared of her." John chuckled slightly as he sat down and began eating. "I still don't know what they're going to be able to do."

"I don't know, either, but the more people we get behind us, the better off we are." I know it sounded lame, but I was running out of ideas. "Have you thought about hiring a lawyer?" I asked, and John nodded as he swallowed.

"I went to Legal Aid, and they just shook their heads. The advice I got from them was to try to work with social services." John set his sandwich back on the plate and pushed it away. "I looked into hiring another lawyer, but I really can't afford it."

"If this doesn't work, we'll find one," I told him. "Those kids need to be with their family."

"Even with this job, I still can't afford one, and if I use all the money I have saved on a lawyer, social services will use that against me somehow." John banged his hand lightly on the snack bar. "I'm between a rock and a hard place, with no way out." I understood John's frustration, and when I'd offered the idea, I'd meant that I'd help him with the fees. I had money saved, but John was proud, and I knew he wouldn't take money from me unless he had no choice.

"Hey, I'm here," I said softly, resting my hand on John's. "You aren't alone. You have your family to help you, your friends and colleagues are behind you, and I'll do whatever I can to help you."

"I know," John said softly. "Thank you."

"You're welcome," I told him, and then I slowly pushed the plate back in front of him before returning to my own lunch. When we were both done, I took care of the dishes.

"I need to take care of some things at home," John said as he stood up and walked toward the front door.

"Of course. Will I see you later?" I got the distinct feeling that John needed some time alone.

"Yes. If it's okay, I'll come back later this afternoon and we can do something together. I need some time to... think, I guess," John answered, rubbing the back of his neck with his hand.

I took a step closer. "You take the time you need. I've got things I need to do around here too." Not that I'd been particularly looking forward to washing the windows, but it definitely needed to be done. "Stop back when you're ready. I was thinking that this afternoon we could check out the water park just outside town. It's supposed to be hot, so water slides and swimming pools might be fun." I had thought it was a good suggestion, but John's expression darkened slightly.

"Maybe we could find something to do without so many children," he said, and I wanted to kick myself. I really hadn't thought that through. "Maybe we can do something quiet."

"Okay," I told him and tugged him into a light kiss. "I'll see you later."

John turned and opened the front door but didn't step outside. "In case I haven't said it properly, I really appreciate everything you've done for me and for the kids." Without waiting for a response, John left. Not having an excuse to put it off any longer, I went upstairs to change into cool clothes and then got all the things together that I'd need to wash the outside windows.

I stuck to the shady side of the house, because in the sun I would bake to a crisp. Setting the ladder against the side of the house, I began with the second-story windows.

The muggy heat surrounded me as I got to work, washing the windows with hot, soapy water and then rinsing them with the hose before squeegeeing them dry. In some cases I had to move the ladder after each window, and in some places I was able to wash multiple windows. After I'd finished about half of them, I peered around as I felt the hair on the back of my neck stand up. Nothing seemed out of place, so I went back to work, only to get the same unsettling feeling once again. I had no idea where it was coming from, and I continued working, finishing the upper windows on that side of the house before washing the lower ones. On the ground I didn't experience that feeling like I was being watched, and I was able to finish the rest of the windows. Then I moved to the back of the house and climbed the ladder once again.

I spent much of the afternoon climbing and descending the ladder. John called up as I was finishing the windows on the front of the house, with only the one side remaining. I was never so pleased to be done with a chore in my life. My legs ached and my back hurt as I descended the ladder for the last time. Looking down, I saw John standing at the base of the ladder, grinning at me. "That's quite a sight," John commented as I stepped onto the grass, setting my things beside the ladder.

I looked around one more time. "I've had the feeling I've been watched all afternoon, and I don't know why. I kept looking around and never saw anyone."

"It could be your imagination, or the fact that your neighbor"—John tilted his head toward Mr. Hooper's house—"is sitting upstairs watching you out of his window." I didn't look right away, but turned to scan around me and caught sight of him sitting up there.

"Old kook," I mumbled, and I began carrying the cleaning supplies back toward the garage. John gave me a hand with the ladder, and soon everything was put away. I could barely walk by the time we reached the front porch. Gingerly, I sat down on the old wicker loveseat, letting out a sigh as the muscles running down the back of my legs throbbed. "Shit, would you like something to drink?" I asked, struggling back to my feet.

"I'll get it," John said, and I smiled gratefully and settled back onto the faded cushion. I saw Mr. Hooper step out of his house and sit on his porch.

"You know, you shouldn't let that injun in your house alone. They'll steal anything they can," Mr. Hooper called across the yard, and I glared back at him.

"I thought we already had the conversation about your stupidity," I called back, and he turned away. I could tell he was fuming, but I really didn't care. "Dumbass," I murmured under my breath as the front door opened and John brought glasses and the pitcher of tea from the refrigerator. "Perfect, thank you," I said, and John set them down. I poured a glass for each of us. "Did you work things through?" I took a sip of the tea.

"No," John replied. "I keep looking for some cause, the one thing that will make everything work right."

I chuckled because I recognized the mindset. "This isn't a computer program, and there isn't necessarily a logical cause."

John set down his glass. "I know. It's based upon someone's judgment and how they feel and apply the rules. It's maddening, because half the time it makes no sense." I couldn't have agreed more and was about to say so when John's phone rang. I took another drink of tea and listened as he talked to what I presumed was his mother. They talked for a while, and I reclined on the seat, trying to find a comfortable position for my back. I finally succeeded as John hung up the phone. "Mom said that the council will meet next Friday to hear what I have to say. I'll have to spend the night, and then I can visit the kids on the way home."

I turned my head so I could see him. "It's quite a drive."

"Yes." I saw John shift in his chair. "You don't have to go with me. It's a lot of driving, and you'll miss quite a bit of work on what could be a completely useless trip."

"If you don't want me to go, just say so," I said, feeling a bit hurt but trying to keep it out of my voice. If John didn't want me with him, that was his business. I didn't know—maybe nontribal people weren't allowed. Or maybe John just didn't want me to go. I turned away and carefully sipped my tea.

John's chair squeaked and then footsteps sounded on the porch floor. "It's not that I don't want you to go," John said, and I scooted over so he could sit on the edge of the seat, next to my legs. "It's a long drive and a lot of time away. I don't want you to feel obligated."

I rolled my eyes at John. "I know we haven't known each other long, but I rarely offer to do anything I don't want to do. If my coming along is going to cause trouble or problems with your family, then I'll stay here, though. Otherwise, I have no intention of letting you do this on your own. I figure I can declare Friday a holiday, and Bryce can have the day off too. We'll have to make up the work, but we can do that as long as we plan for it. And on the way back, we can stop in Chamberlain and see the kids." My mind was already beginning to work out what we'd need to do and the extra hours I'd need to put in to make sure we got everything done.

"If you're sure," John said.

"I'm sure," I told him with conviction, even as I was still trying to figure out how to get all the work done in time, but I'd worked long hours before, and I could do it again.

I placed my glass on the table, and John helped me carry the things inside. I heard him moving around the kitchen as I settled on the sofa, my eyes already closing. I felt John sit next to me, and I cracked my eyes open as he kissed me.

"I don't know what to say," John said as he brushed my hair out of my eyes. I knew what I wanted John to say, because I'd come to realize as I was climbing up and down that damned ladder that everything was more fun, even tedious chores, if John was doing them with me. The beautiful man with the deep eyes and long, jet-black hair was quickly working his way into my heart. As John kissed me again, I wound my arms around his neck, deepening the kiss. I was a goner; I knew that. With each kiss I fell deeper and deeper. I could feel in the way John threw himself into the kiss that he felt something as well, but exactly what, I wasn't sure.

CHAPTER

# SEVEN

THE week was hard. I told Bryce about taking Friday and Saturday off and gave him the opportunity to take them off as well, so all three of us worked long hours beginning at seven in the morning and not quitting until almost six. We got a great deal accomplished, and by Thursday night we were well ahead, and Bryce assured us he fully intended to enjoy his long weekend, even as he stifled a yawn as he left the office. Peter had even stopped by after work a few times, finishing what he'd been working on, and I was able to show him some of the more advanced spreadsheet functions. After closing up tightly, I made a light dinner, and then John and I fell into bed, sleeping soundly until the alarm went off at a god-awful hour of the morning.

By seven in the morning on Friday, John and I were on the freeway heading toward the far side of the state. The trip to Rapid City was about three hundred miles, and thankfully the freeway speed limit was seventy-five, so we were able to make excellent time. We hit Rapid City for lunch and a gas fill-up before turning south toward Hot Springs. From there, we took smaller roads into the reservation. This part of the state was completely unfamiliar to me, and I had to rely on John to give me directions. "This is a lot of effort for what could be a fool's errand," John said as we carefully traversed the rough road that led us deeper into the reservation.

"We're expected at two?" I asked as my teeth rattled from all the bumps. "How much farther is it?" As soon as I asked the question, we hit a paved road and we were able to speed up.

"About ten more miles and we should be at the tribal center," John explained. We'd spelled each other driving and each of us had napped along the way, but my legs ached from hours in the car, and all I wanted was to get out and walk around for a while. Instead, I drove and peered out the window as small groups of what looked like ramshackle houses and trailers passed by outside. Some were in better condition than others. I hadn't quite known what to expect, but this was eye-opening.

"There isn't much work here," John explained as though he were reading my mind. "And it's not like there's traffic that runs through the res. If there was, we could probably build a casino, like many tribes have, but there isn't even that." The sadness in his voice was palpable.

"The scenery is beautiful, though, with the Black Hills in the distance."

"Those mountains are sacred to my people," John told me, and I nodded.

"I know," was all I could think to say. The tribes still disputed the ownership of the mountains and held old treaties with the government that they claimed had been broken. I tended to believe them, but the federal government held a very different view. Eventually we came to what looked like a small town, and John had me park outside the largest building.

"This is the tribal center," John explained, and I nodded. I got out of the car and followed John as he walked inside. I wasn't sure what I had been expecting. Maybe something more traditional, but it was a relatively modern small government building.

"Akecheta," a woman called, and then he was engulfed in the arms of a middle-aged woman with a round face and warm, ruddy cheeks. They spoke rapidly in Lakota, greeting each other warmly. John looked a great deal like his mother, but it was her eyes that drew me in, the same way John's always did.

"Mom, this is Jerry," John said, introducing me. To say she looked at me skeptically was a huge understatement. "Jerry, this is my mother, Kiya."

"It's a pleasure to meet you," I said and extended my hand. I honestly didn't know if she would take it or ignore me. John said something, and she extended her hand, shaking mine briefly before turning to John and saying something I didn't understand. John said something in return, but his tone was unmistakable.

"Jerry has been a huge help," John went on to explain in English. "He gave me a good job, and he's written letters and driven me to see the kids. He even closed the office so we could come here today." I noticed that he didn't say anything about the rest of our relationship, and I reminded myself to ask him about that when we were alone so I wouldn't say anything inappropriate. "Jerry has been a very good friend to me and to Mato and Ichante."

"They've met him?" she asked, and John turned away from me, firing off what sounded like rapid-fire Lakota. I watched as Kiya's expression softened before my eyes. I looked around and noticed a few folding chair near the wall. Sitting down, I waited for them to finish talking. I knew I was the subject of their conversation, and while I couldn't understand a word, John's aggressive posture with his mother told me all I needed to know. When they were done, John walked over to where I sat.

"Please forgive us," he said to me. "I know it was rude, but there were things I needed to make sure were cleared up." He looked back at his mother, and she nodded, looking a bit chastised, even as her gaze traveled over John and then to me. "The council will be ready for us in about half an hour," John said, and he took the chair next to mine. Eventually, John's mother sat next to him, and they talked quietly. People came and went, some stopping to speak briefly to John. In their own time, someone came out and called us in.

I was half expecting some sort of grand entrance, but instead we were led into a room that reminded me of the last time I'd gone to a city council meeting, except the walls were painted with what I imagined were traditional scenes and the men were gathered in a circle with space left for people to approach. Some were dressed in sports coats, while other council members wore what looked to be more traditional clothing and jewelry. Almost every one of the men had long hair tied in a braid. "Akecheta Black Raven," one of the men said as he stood up and greeted John. Then all eyes in the room focused on me, and John introduced me and briefly explained why I was here. I half expected to be asked to leave, but John directed me to a chair before he approached the council.

"I am here to ask the council's help in securing the return of Mato and Ichante Black Raven. At the death of my sister, they were placed in the care of child services, and I have been trying for seven months to get custody of them. They are living with a white family in Chamberlain, away from our people and our culture. Their hair has been cut, and they know almost nothing of our ways, except what little they remember of what my sister taught them before her death." John paused, and I saw the tribal leaders looking at each other and nodding. Somehow I didn't think this was the first time they had heard stories like this. John went on to describe his fight to see the kids as well as all the obstacles that had been placed in his way. He motioned to me. "I have a good job, thanks to Jerry Lincoln taking a chance when I was new out of school and hiring me. I also have a place to live and can support and care for Mato and Ichante. Furthermore, I have members of our people who are willing to assist in their care and to help me teach them our ways."

"May I ask," one of the older council members asked, his face thick with wrinkles that looked as though he'd seen many hardships and disappointments, his hair, long and gray. "What is this man to you?"

John looked at me and then back toward the council. "He is someone I care a great deal for and the one I hope to be with for a long time," John answered, and I felt the eyes of everyone on the council turn to me. I knew I could look away like I was ashamed or face them, so I looked them all squarely back, not looking away until they did. "I am asking the council's help and support in my quest for the return of my sister's children," John continued, bringing the council's attention back to him, "the grandchildren of Kiya and Wamblee Black Raven, Mato and Ichante Black Raven."

John stood still for a few seconds and then stepped back from the council. "We will need to deliberate this issue," the man who'd spoken earlier said, and John turned to leave the room. I followed, as did John's mother, closing the door behind us.

"They're going to talk about this until they're blue in the face, but will they do anything?" I knew John's question was rhetorical, and I watched as he paced the room. I'd learned it was what he did when he was nervous and upset.

"Do you think they will take a while?" I asked his mother, and she looked toward the chamber and nodded, but said nothing.

"Would you like to take a walk?" I asked John, and he nodded, already at the door. I followed, and we went out into the nearly stifling afternoon heat. "Is there anything around to see?"

"There's the missionary store," John answered, and he began walking across the gravel parking area, past what looked like a small school with old playground equipment behind it, and up to a small blue-gray building with a white door. John pushed it open, and we stepped inside. There was no air-conditioning, and the heat inside was almost as bad as the air outside, but at least we were out of the sun.

A small woman sat behind the desk, and she looked up from her book to smile at John before returning to what she was doing. The walls were lined with shelves. On one side were inexpensive religious items, pamphlets, and booklets, along with a few shelves of basic necessities. On the other side were handicrafts and carvings. "The missionaries give artisans a place to sell their goods," John explained, and I looked at the intricate baskets, handwoven blankets, and wood carvings. I picked up one of the baskets with weaving so fine you could barely see it, and peered at the price before setting it back down. It was remarkable.

John seemed nervous and anxious to get back. I motioned toward the door, and we stepped back out into the sun. "You look about ready to pounce on someone at any second."

"This was a wasted trip," John snapped as he strode back toward the tribal center, and I struggled to keep up. "There's nothing any of us can do. Mato and Ichante are at the mercy of the ugly white woman, and the sooner I realize that and play her game, the sooner I can get them back." John didn't turn to go inside, but continued walking around the building. "I should have been there. The white people never would have gotten the kids if I'd have been there with her." I knew John was upset and needed a chance to burn off some of the energy and the feelings of uselessness.

"John, guilt doesn't help," I said, and that stopped him. "All it does is take something bad and make it worse." John didn't respond, but started walking again, and I followed him. This time, when we reached the front of the building, he went inside and sat next to his mother. I took a chair next to him and sat with my eyes glued to the door to the council chamber.

After a while, the door opened and we were ushered back inside. John approached the council, and I went to sit where I had before.

"Akecheta Black Raven, we have heard your words and your story is not new to us," said the older man who'd spoken before. "Many of the children of this tribe and others of our nation have suffered as Mato and Ichante do. We have decided that it is time to fight." The others on the council nodded their agreement, and I wondered exactly what they meant. "We have authorized the attorney for the tribe to initiate proceeding to file charges in the kidnapping of Mato and Ichante Black Raven against child services and the state of South Dakota."

I nearly gasped and had to stop myself from making a sound. John's mother did gasp, and then she hurried to John and stood beside him.

"Thank you," John said. "I have information I can provide to the attorney regarding all the things I have done to try to get my niece and nephew back." John looked over at me. "Jerry helped me get everything together and made sure I kept all the original documents."

The council members looked to me, and I stood and stepped forward. "As John said, we have all recent documents, and we have approximate dates of all other interactions. I can give further testimony on how child services tried to keep John from seeing the children even as the foster parents were wondering why he didn't visit. They were purposely keeping John away from those children using deception and lies."

Council members began talking among themselves, and then the man who'd done the speaking in the past—probably the council leader, although I wasn't sure—spoke directly to me. "Why are you helping John and us?"

# THE GOOD FIGHT

I looked at John and then back at the council. "Why wouldn't I?" I had no context to answer their question. "I'm sorry, but I don't understand your question." Then it hit me. "Please forgive my potential rudeness, and know it is not intentional, but I have a neighbor who's a complete idiot, and he told me that I shouldn't let John go into my house alone because that 'injun'"—I made air quotes—"would steal from me. Now, my idiot neighbor is closed-minded and prejudiced, and I suspect if he really understood that John and I were dating and interested in each other as more than friends, he'd probably call both of us much worse."

"Is there a point?" the leader asked.

"Yes. Isn't your question the same as my idiot neighbor's, just from the other perspective? You asked me why I would help John get custody of his niece and nephew, and I assume you're asking because I'm white, but isn't that the same prejudice my neighbor used on John?" I saw the council members look at one another. "I'm helping John because it's the right thing to do. Those children need a good home, and John can give them that. I also care for John and want him to be happy. Is there any better reason?" I stopped talking because I figured they were probably about to lynch me, especially as the murmurs continued.

"We have many reasons for being distrustful of outsiders, and I wanted to understand your motives," he explained. "We meant no disrespect."

"I didn't either," I said, and I lowered my eyes slightly, saying nothing more.

"Akecheta, you know what you have chosen will not be met with acceptance by all the people. Some, including members of this council, will not understand you being with another man, white or not," the leader said.

John stole a look at me. "I must be true to myself, and that's what our tradition dictates, as well." John paused for a moment.

"I'll expect to hear from the tribal lawyers." John turned and walked toward the back of the chamber, with myself and his mother following behind. As soon as the door closed, Kiya hugged John jubilantly.

"You have the entire tribe behind you now," she said before looking at me. "I see what my son means to you and what you mean to him." She studied me for a few seconds. "We'll see," she added a bit cryptically, and I looked at John, who shrugged. I guess I still had something to prove to her. With that, she turned and walked toward the outside door. "I'll expect both of you for dinner."

"As long as it's early, Mom," John cautioned. "We have to get back to Rapid City tonight, and to Chamberlain before lunch tomorrow so we can see the kids."

"I'll start home and begin cooking." She obviously wasn't taking no for an answer, and we followed her out and to the car. She pulled out of the parking lot, and I drove over to the store.

"I want that basket that I saw earlier," I explained to John, and I hurried inside. The woman was still behind the counter, reading, and I picked up the basket and brought it to her. "I'd like this, please. Do you take credit cards?"

She looked at me like I was from another planet. "No, I'm sorry."

"A check, then? I'm with Akecheta Black Raven," I explained.

"Of course," she told me, and I hurried back to the car, rummaged in the glove compartment for my checkbook, and then stepped back inside the store. She figured the amount, and I wrote her a check. After packing up the basket, she wrote me a receipt, and I thanked her.
"You're welcome," she said as I left the store, carrying my

purchase. After placing it on the back seat, I pulled away from the store and followed John's directions to his mother's house.

"Did you really buy the basket?" John asked.

"Of course. It's beautiful, handmade, and I hope the sale will help someone on the reservation."

"It will," John said, and I wondered what his expression meant, but before I could ask, it was gone.

"I'm going to need directions to your mother's," I said, and John directed me. We wound through the reservation, and I knew for sure that I'd never find my way back to the main road once we actually got to his mother's house. "You aren't trying to get me hopelessly lost so you can have your way with me, are you?"

John slid his hand lightly along my thigh. "I don't think I need to get you lost for that," John said, snickering, and I groaned. The last thing I wanted was to arrive at his mother's for dinner sporting wood, but the way John was teasing me made that a real possibility. "Slow down and turn off right here," John instructed, and I slowed down, pulling into what looked like an old driveway. I turned to John and stopped the car as the track appeared to end.

"What are you doing?" I asked with a laugh as I put the car into park. John leaned across the seat and tugged me into a kiss.

"Having my way with you," John said, his voice deepening before he kissed me with all the pent-up energy he'd been holding back. I heard the car engine go quiet and realized John had turned it off. He pressed his weight to me as he slipped a hand under my shirt. I squirmed and whined softly as John lightly tweaked a nipple. I arched into the touch as he made small circles beneath my shirt.

"John," I gaped, carding my fingers through his long, silken hair. "This isn't a good idea." My dick, on the other hand, throbbing and straining in my pants, thought this was an amazingly fantastic idea. John seemed to sense that as well, because I felt him work open my pants, and the zipper on my jeans slid down. I breathed a sigh of relief as the constraints fell away. I thrust forward, unable to stop myself, and I heard John chuckle as he pressed my shirt up my chest. Then I felt him tug at the waistband of my briefs, pulling them down. My cock sprang free, and I released a deep guttural moan that seemed to come from my toes.

My ass slid forward in the seat, and I gasped for breath as I felt John's cheek slide down my stomach. Looking down, all I could see was John's head in my lap, his hair draping around my legs. But what I felt was something else entirely: hot, firm lips surrounded me, sliding slowly down my length as John sucked me into his mouth, slow and deep. I began whimpering as I tried to thrust deeper, but John stilled me with a light touch on my leg.

I pressed his head lower, and I felt John stop. Then he took my hands in his, transferring them to the steering wheel, and I white-knuckled the thing as he took me to the root. "Jesus Christ!" I screamed, and my voice filled the confined space. I couldn't help thrusting, lifting my butt off the seat. Once I did, I felt John's hand glide along my thigh, then a finger pressed to my opening, and I swore even louder. "Please, John." I begged and pleaded, but he knew exactly how to hold me at bay, balancing me on the head of a pin so that the slightest bit of extra pressure would send me over, but he didn't. John held me there as my legs bounced and my cock jumped and throbbed in his mouth. No matter what I tried to do, nothing would let me tumble into the sweet oblivion of release until John let me. I rolled my head back and forth on the headrest, everything outside the car fading away as I watched John slowly bob his head along my length.

I let loose a strangled cry when John pulled back, letting me slip from his lips. "John!" My entire body thrummed with energy it couldn't contain; my arms and legs shook, I was nearly seeing double—and he was pulling away. He leaned over me, and I felt the back of my seat recline.

"Close your eyes," John commanded, pressing his finger inside me for added emphasis, and I pressed them shut, vibrating with anticipation. Gripping the seat tight, I waited for what John had in mind. "Lift your hips," he whispered, and I complied, feeling my pants slide down my legs to my ankles.

Something tickled my skin, lightly sending my nerves jumping. At first I couldn't figure out what it was, but then I gasped and gripped the base of the seat as I realized it was John's hair. "Fuck me," I groaned, thrusting my hips forward.

"Later, when I get you back to the hotel," John whispered, and I felt his hair move around my cock in slow circles. I swallowed hard and fought the urge to open my eyes. "I'm going to take you to heaven and hold you there for hours," John promised, and I gripped the seat tighter. The light tickles faded away, and John swallowed me down hard, his lips gripping me like a vise. Lifting my hips once more, thrusting with abandon, I felt John press his finger deep inside me. When he rubbed the spot inside me, I came unglued, thrusting hard and fast as my release boiled up from deep inside me. I came with a near ear-piercing scream that shook the windows.

Flopping back on the seat, I gasped for breath as I slipped from John's mouth. I tried to open my eyes, but they didn't seem to work. "What about you?" I mumbled, and I heard John's soft chuckles as he withdrew from my body.

"I'll wait until we get to the hotel," John said, and I was finally able to crack my eyes open.

"But...," I protested, leaning forward, but John pressed me back with a soft touch.

"There's nothing hotter or more beautiful than when I bring you over the edge," John said. Somehow I doubted that, because

I'd seen him in the throes of passion, but I didn't have the energy to argue. All I could do was breathe for a while until heat began to build up in the car. Opening my eyes, all I saw were fogged windows and John smiling at me like the cat who'd swallowed the canary.

"What's that for?" I asked as I began pulling my clothes back into place.

"You look completely debauched," John told me.

"This coming from the debaucher himself." I snickered as I lifted my butt off the seat so I could pull my pants into place. After pulling down my shirt, I made sure I looked reasonably put together before getting my seat back into position.

I was about to start the car when John placed his hand on mine, and as I turned toward him, he kissed me as gently and as sweetly as he ever had. "Thank you for all you've done for me and my family."

"You're welcome," I answered, starting the car. I waited for the windows to clear, and then we continued on toward John's mother's house.

"Are you ready to meet my family?" John asked as he had me make another turn.

"After that, I'm ready to meet your family and half the Sioux nation." My head still swam.

"Meeting my family will probably feel like meeting half the Sioux nation, believe me," John countered before instructing me to turn into a driveway. John had me pull up to a large, old house with a yard filled with playing children. I parked, and as soon as we opened the door, the sound of laughter and screams of excited joy assaulted me. It had been a long time since I'd been around a large group of children.

"I see what you mean," I said as I saw a stream of people walking to and from the house, setting up tables in the shade of a huge old tree, and then carrying out food and dishes. "Who are these people?"

"Brothers, sisters, cousins, aunts, uncles—you name it, they're all here. I suspect that Mom put out the call as soon as she knew we were coming, and no one ignores a summons from Kiya," John explained just before he was surrounded by a passel of kids, all vying for his attention.

"Akecheta!" they yelled, some jumping up and down. He picked up each of the littler ones in turn, getting hugs from them all. I heard one of the small boys whisper rather loudly, as boys do, "Who's the white man?"

"This is a good friend of mine. His name is Jerry, and he's been helping me try to get Mato and Ichante back. So be nice to him," John said with a smile, and the little boy in his arms was passed to me. He looked almost as startled as I felt. "That's Kohana," John explained.

"Are you going to eat me?" Kohana asked, his eyes wide.

"Who told you that?" I asked, and he pointed to one of the older boys.

"No," I told him with a smile. "But I might eat him if he's mean to you." I gave him a wink that set him to a fit of giggles, and when I set him down, he raced away toward the other kids, smacking the older boy in question before running back to me. "I guess I made a friend," I told John as I lifted Kohana back into my arms.

"Come on," John said with a chuckle. "Let's go meet everyone."

I looked toward the tables and then back at John. "Can't I stay with the kids?" There were so many people, and they were all looking at me. John led me to the group and began making introductions. I lost track of names and relationships after three people. One of the women took Kohana from my arms, and I lost

123

my shield. My hand was shaken, and I was greeted so many times I thought my head would spin.

"Where's your father?" I asked John once the introductions were over.

"He's in North Dakota with a group of the other men and a few women from the tribe. They're working in the oil fields up there. He comes home about once a month or so," John told me. "There's no work here, so they go where they can find it." I nodded my understanding and suppressed a sigh as more food was brought out, and Kiya called everyone to the huge tables.

John sat down, and I was about to as well when Kohana insinuated himself between us with a grin. Bowls of food were passed around, the adults helping the children. John and I helped Kohana. Then everyone began to eat. The conversation never stilled for a second. Everyone talked and laughed as they ate. It was one huge family, and they acted as close as I'd ever seen this large a group of people. Some of the food was familiar, but other dishes were new, and I tried them all. Occasionally I saw one of the women smile when I took a bite and I realized I was eating her dish. There was wohanpi, a traditional soup—more like a stew—of bison meat, and fry bread, as well as green salads and cooked greens.

"What do you do?" the woman across the table from me asked, and the conversation seemed to still. I couldn't for the life of me remember her name, but I believed she was one of John's cousins.

"Computer consulting. John and I work together," I explained. "We develop complex web applications for our clients." I wasn't sure how much information to give.

"Jerry is teaching me a lot," John explained. "I'm working on projects for companies all over the country."

"You should teach computers here," she said and looked down the table to the others, who nodded their agreement.

"Jerry lives in Sioux Falls, and that's where his business is," John said, and the conversation moved on. I didn't realize it at the time, but the seed of an idea had been planted.

CHAPTER
# EIGHT

WE ARRIVED in Rapid City very late. Thank God John knew the roads well, because until we reached the freeway, everything looked the same to me. We finally made it, though, pulling into the hotel parking lot just off the freeway a little after midnight. We were both so tired we could barely move, and after checking into our room, we both fell into bed. So how on earth John could be up at six in the morning was beyond me, but he was.

"Wake me in an hour," I mumbled before burying my head in the pillow. I easily fell back to sleep and only woke when I felt the covers slide away and John's hot tongue on my back, moving down toward my butt. I groaned, instantly hard, as John slowly slid a finger inside me. "Yeah," I groaned with my eyes still closed. I was only half-awake, but it was obviously the good half, if what John was making me feel was any indication. One finger became two, and then they slipped away. I heard movement and knew John was getting ready for the main event.

John pressed his cock to my opening, and I pressed back against him as he slowly entered my body. I stretched, my hands pushing against the headboard as he sank into me, every nerve and muscle suddenly waking and springing to life. "Good?" John asked as he settled his weight on top of me, his chest to my back as he nuzzled at the base of my neck.

"Oh yeah," I moaned softly. "Fuck me."

"I will, baby," John teased as he flexed his hips slightly, his cock rubbing that perfect place. "Like that?" he whispered as he did it again.

"Yeah," I groaned, fisting the pillow as he slowly withdrew and then pushed back into me. Nothing on earth felt better than John filling me. It was like he had been made for me: long and just wide enough to stretch and fill without hurting. "That's it, right there!" I cried into the pillow as John steadily picked up the pace. John wrapped his arms around my chest, plucking my nipples as he held me close, snapping his hips to drive deep. "That's what I want," I told him, and he drove deeper, quickening his pace as he ground my hips and dick into the bedding. With each thrust, my cock rubbed against the sheets, providing the perfect amount of friction.

"Been hard all night," John whispered into my ear. "Been thinking of you and how good it feels to make love to you." John pegged my gland, and I damned near saw stars. "Lay awake staring at the ceiling thinking about this."

I whimpered as I felt my climax already starting to build. Between John filling my ass and his words filling my ears, there was no way I could last very long, and John drove into me, bouncing us both on the bed as I came hard with John throbbing deep inside me.

John rested on top of me, and I lowered my head to the pillow, enjoying the feel of his weight. After a few minutes, I felt him move off me and then settle on the bed, tugging me close. Closing my eyes, I drifted back to sleep, not waking until I felt John shift and get out of bed. I knew we needed to leave, but after the driving, the dinner, and all the noise from John's family, I relished the peace and quiet of the hotel room.

"We need to get going," John whispered into my ear, and I groggily got out of bed and padded to the bathroom to try to wake up. A quick shower, shave, and cleanup later, I got dressed and then we walked down to the lobby. The strong coffee from the hotel coffeemaker did the trick, and I finally began to push sleep away. After breakfast, we checked out of the hotel and packed the car before heading down the freeway. John drove and I slept, waking as we passed through Wall and entered the plains. I took over driving after a while, and we pulled into Chamberlain and up to the Caruthers's house a little before noon. The kids must have been watching for us, because they bounded out, happily embracing both of us as we got out of the car.

"Good morning, Mary," I called as she stepped out of the house. She smiled and walked down the drive to meet us. "How are you doing?"

"Just fine," she answered and led us into the house. John greeted her as well. Compared to our first couple of visits, John was now much less tense, but I did see him touch both Mato and Ichante's hair. I knew the length and the fact that it had been cut bothered him a great deal. But to his credit, he kept quiet because he didn't want to cause trouble. "Come inside," she offered, as she always did, and we followed her. As always, she brought out a tray with lemonade and glasses. She and I talked while John played and talked with the kids.

"Is he making any progress with child services?" Mary asked. "Not that I want to get rid of them," she added, looking at Mato and Ichante. "They're wonderful kids, and I'd adopt them if I could. But they need to be with family."

"We're not sure," I answered. If John wanted her to know what was going on, then that was his story to tell, not mine. "I know he's making progress."

"When I was contacted the last time, I told them that John had been visiting regularly, and that he took good care of them and it was clear he cared deeply for them." Mary sipped from her glass. "I hope that was okay."

"It was very kind of you. I really appreciate it," John said as he came over.

We stayed for a while, with the kids showing John their toys and just spending some time with him. When the kids got hungry, we took them and Mary to lunch in town before once again saying good-bye and driving back to Sioux Falls. John was quiet for a lot of the trip. I drove, and he stared out the passenger window. I knew exactly what he was thinking. Every time he left the kids, John felt as though he might not see them again. He'd told me that a few times, and now that the tribe was going to take some action, he could feel some hope, though that made the parting even more bittersweet because impatience was kicking in. I could see a glimmer of light at the end of the tunnel, and I knew John could as well. That had to be working his patience badly. "You were right," John finally said. "It was very nice of her to say those things."

"I told you she wasn't your enemy, and by cultivating her friendship, you may have someone else who can help you." John was quiet for a while again, and I just drove, letting the miles tick by.

"How long do you think it will be until they file the suit?" John asked. "And do you really think it will help?" I could hear both the hope and the doubt in his voice.

"Sometimes these things are about getting someone's attention, and once charges are brought, the media will get involved, and child services will want to defuse the situation as quickly as possible," I explained.

"What if they decide to fight?" John asked.

"I'm not a lawyer, but it seems to me that if they fight, they run the risk of losing, and that would undermine them even more.

129

I suspect they'll try to make this go away as quickly and quietly as possible, but you never know." I returned to my driving and left John alone with his thoughts.

By the time we arrived at the house, we were both exhausted. When I pulled into the driveway, I was surprised to see Bryce's car parked off to the side. I parked next to him and got out, then went around the house to the office. Opening the door, I saw Bryce and Peter sitting at the table, talking. "I thought you'd take the day off. What are you doing here?" I asked, stepping into the office with John behind me.

"I was going to, but Peter called and asked if I could help him with the records," Bryce said, and I looked at Peter, who seemed unusually pleased.

"I got this done, and with Bryce's help, it's organized the way you wanted it," Peter said proudly. "I also realized that this isn't for me. I'm glad I took the time to learn some things, but this type of work isn't what I'm good at."

"Okay," I said, trying to hide my relief. By my calculations, Peter had taken about seven hours or so to do four hours of work. "At least you picked up a skill you didn't have before." Peter was very much a people person, and I had sort of figured he'd go a bit stir-crazy working at a computer all day, but he'd done a lot to help me, so I was willing to try to help him.

Bryce was shutting down his workstation, and then he shut down the computer Peter had been using as well. "How was your trip?" he asked as he closed the lid on the laptop, and I let John answer.

"The council listened to my story and said it was one they were familiar with." John walked to where I was standing. "The council decided to take action, and they've instructed their lawyer to gather the facts needed to file charges of kidnapping against the state." Peter whistled, and Bryce looked shocked, but neither said anything. "I suspect the lawyer will be in touch pretty soon."

John yawned, and I followed right behind him. We'd been driving for what seemed like the better part of two days.

"I'll see you Monday," I told Bryce as he went to leave. "Have fun with Percy."

"I will," Bryce called and hurried away. Peter said he had to leave as well, and I locked up the office. After saying good-bye to Peter, we headed inside.

"You hungry?" I asked, and John shook his head.

"I should go on home. I've got things I need to do, and I'm not going to be very good company," John explained with a yawn, and after a good-bye kiss, he picked up his overnight bag and left the house. I wondered why he was making a hasty retreat, but got my things from the car and went upstairs to put the clothes away before returning to the living room. I placed the basket I'd purchased on the display shelf and then switched on the television. I fell asleep on the sofa and didn't wake up until I heard my phone. The room was nearly dark as I fumbled around on the coffee table.

"Hey, John," I answered with a yawn.

"Did I wake you?" he asked, and I looked at the clock—a little before ten.

"Yeah, but I probably should have gotten up hours ago."

"I was sitting around here doing nothing, wishing I was with you, and I figured I was being stupid, so I thought I'd call."

"Is that the long way of saying you want to come over?" I asked as I sat up. "Where are you?" My doorbell rang, and I chuckled as I heard it through the phone too. "Well, come in," I told him, and then I hung up the phone. The door opened and John came inside with a grin. "You know, you didn't have to go earlier," I told John once we were sitting together on the sofa after a deep hello kiss.

131

"I didn't want to wear out my welcome. We'd been together for two days, and I thought you might have wanted some time by yourself," John explained.

"If I had, I would have told you, I promise," I said, tugging him closer. "I've had plenty of time alone. If you want me to be honest, what I really like is the time I spend with you." I leaned closer, inhaling John's rich scent and running my fingers through his hair as I kissed him. John responded by pressing me back on the cushions. The living room sofa had already seen plenty of action lately and more was in store. "Did you mean what you said this morning in the hotel?"

John stopped his kissing, and I wondered if I'd gone too far. John's words had hovered at the edge of my mind ever since we left the hotel, but now I wondered if they had just been a slip of the tongue. "What did I say?" John asked, each measured word increasing my worry. I knew I should have just kept my mouth shut.

"You said we were making love." There, I'd said it, and I half expected John to run screaming from the house or at least make excuses about how it had been in the heat of the moment and that what was said then didn't count. I'd actually been told that once before, by Carlos, the asshole. And I so didn't want to hear that now.

"We were making love," John told me as he pressed closer. "We always make love when we're together." Then he kissed me, and everything else stopped except him.

"Is that how you really feel?" I asked, not wanting to let myself believe what I thought John was saying, even as my heart leaped at the prospect.

"Yes, that's how I feel," John replied, his gaze boring into me, and I realized the usually intensely strong man was looking for confirmation that I felt the same way. John's vulnerability was palpably visible in his swirling eyes. I gave him all the confirmation he could possibly want by pulling him into a hard kiss and practically devouring his mouth, my tongue subduing John's to take possession of him. "I take it you feel the same," John groaned when I broke the kiss, his eyes a bit unfocused.

"Yes. I've felt that way for a while but wasn't sure how you felt, so—" I was cut off by an equally intense kiss from John that curled my toes.

"Let's take this upstairs. I'm tired of this couch, and I want to make love to you in a proper bed where you'll have plenty of room to stretch out as I fill you so full you'll scream yourself hoarse." My head throbbed. John certainly had a way with words when he wanted to. After getting up, he stood next to the couch and extended his hand, and tugged me to my feet. Then he led me up the stairs and into the bedroom, where he did exactly what he'd promised, and so very much more.

CHAPTER
# NINE

THE lawyer called John the following Monday, and we spent the next several evenings putting together and organizing materials to send to him, along with as much detail as we could possibly provide. He then came to Sioux Falls and met with us. I provided a deposition as to what I knew regarding Mary Caruthers's sentiments and surprise. Most of what I knew was from what John had told me, so I was little help other than keeping John from exploding as his patience thinned. The days had turned into a week with no word, and then into two. John had gotten as nervous as a cat in a room full of rocking chairs, as my grandmother used to say when I was a kid.

Finally, more than two weeks after returning to the reservation, and after another visit with the kids that left John even more depressed and frustrated when he had to leave them, he got a call at work that the charges had been filed. Sure enough, as we'd hoped, the local news stations picked up on the story and had been broadcasting it all afternoon. The other tribes had joined the chorus of condemnation of the state and child services. But still we heard nothing about the kids from anyone.

"I'm heading home," John said as the workday ground to a close and he shut down his workstation. Bryce had left an hour earlier, so it was just the two of us. John had taken to going home in the evenings so he'd be there in case something changed or someone called. It hadn't done anything up till now except allow him additional time to brood, and I had to say, if brooding became an Olympic sport, John could win the gold medal, hands down.

"I'm going with you," I told him, shutting down my terminal as well, and I motioned him toward the house. I didn't want him to be alone too much, and quite frankly, I was getting tired of being in a relationship with Mr. Broody. He needed something to take his mind off things, and I knew just the thing.

John looked at me skeptically but said nothing, and I hurried upstairs, threw a few things in a small bag, and then followed John to his apartment. It wasn't particularly large, but it was clean and had two bedrooms, one of which had a set of bunk beds ready for Mato and Ichante, complete with a few toys for each of them. I'd been here before, and the apartment struck me the way it always did, like the entire place was holding its breath waiting for something to happen, and in a way it probably was. This was an apartment John had taken and furnished as best he could in anticipation of living here with the kids. That had been months ago, and the inhabitants it had been meant for had yet to come, so everything waited, including John.

After setting my bag in John's room, I joined him in the living room. "It's going to be okay. The waiting is the hardest part."

"I just wish we'd hear something—anything," John almost pleaded. "It's been weeks and nothing's happened. I expected after the news stories something would happen, but nothing."

"It's only been a few days," I soothed, but I knew it wouldn't do much good. The longer this dragged out, the harder it was on John. I knew that, but I didn't know what to do to help him. I'd tried sex, many, many times, and we'd had some interesting results. I still blushed thinking about some of those results. And it wasn't as though I couldn't distract him with sex now. He sat down on the sofa, and I joined him, scooting close. "I don't want to be the bearer of bad news, but I think you need to prepare yourself for a long fight." I could feel John tense next to me. "I'm not saying there will be one, but you need to be prepared for it."

"I don't know how I can be," John told me. "I spend my days and nights thinking about them and the fact that Mato and Ichante should be with their family and not some stranger." John sighed. "They're growing up without all the things I had: cousins, aunts and uncles, the whole extended family—all of that is closed to them right now."

"I know, and it was great meeting your family. Intimidating, but great." My head still spun as I tried to remember who was who.

John turned on the television, and we watched something inane. Or at least I watched it. I could feel John brooding next to me, his arms folded over his chest, occasionally muttering under his breath.

A firm knock on the door an hour later had John nearly jumping out of his skin. "It's okay," I told him, and he walked across the living room, peering outside through the peephole before pulling open the door. Mato and Ichante dropped what they were carrying and ran into his arms, both fighting over who was going to get to hug him first. I peered around him and saw a severe-looking woman standing just outside the door. John showed no interest in moving and simply fell back onto the floor as he hugged both the kids again and again. I could hardly believe my eyes, and I blinked a couple times to make sure what I was seeing was real, so John had to be nearly completely overwhelmed.

"I need to look at the apartment," the woman said, and John lifted Mato into his arms and held Ichante's hand as he guided them inside. "Damn," I said under my breath, "ugly white woman fits." She looked at me, and I stared back at her as she wandered through the apartment.

"You've been here before," John told her sternly and then ignored her as he took the kids down the short hall. "This is your room," he told them, and I heard laughter drift out. "I'll be right back. You need to decide who gets the top bunk," I heard John say, and I smiled. Then he came back into the living room.

"You really should have a bedroom for each child," she said as she wrote on a sheet.

"And you should be in prison for kidnapping!" John snapped. "If I had my way you would be, and you still may be. Just because you delivered the children doesn't mean we're dropping the charges." I got up and stood behind John.

"We've placed the children in your care on a trial basis, and we can remove them at any time," she said without a hint of fear as she walked toward the door. John followed her out, and as soon as she was across the threshold, she turned to say something, and John pressed the door closed, cutting her off mid-word. Then he threw the lock loudly before smiling.

"Mato, Ichante!" he called, and they hurried out. "You get to stay."

I expected cries of happiness, but instead they smiled like they didn't believe it. I heard sounds from outside the door and peered out. Opening the door, I saw bags sitting outside the door, obviously the kid's things, and I brought them in before stepping outside and closing the door behind me to give John some privacy. I walked down the path toward the parking area and saw the social worker pulling grocery bags out of the car.

"Do you need some help?" I asked her as I approached, and she grumbled and placed them in my arms.

"At least you have some manners," she snipped.

"You haven't exactly been helpful," I retorted as she pulled the side door closed on the minivan.

"He'll need to get a car seat for Mato and a booster seat for Ichante," she told me, "and I'll need to check in on the children periodically."

She didn't say anything more before getting in the van, and I turned back toward the apartment with the bags. As I peered into one of them, I saw the doll John had given Ichante, and all I could think was *thank God this is over*. Carrying the bags, I entered a surprisingly quiet apartment and found John with the kids in their room. I took the doll off the top of the bag and handed it to Ichante. She hugged it to her chest, rocking it back and forth. "John, I'm going to go home and leave the three of you alone. You need some time together."

Mato slid off the bed and pawed through one of the bags until he came up with the horse John had given him. Then he raced to me and lifted his arms. I looked at John and then picked him up. I got a hug for my troubles. "I think Mato wants you to stay," John said, and the little boy nodded. "I think they associate you with me since we visited together so often."

At least Mato seemed to. Ichante stood near John and was reluctant to move away. "Did you have dinner?" I asked, and Mato shook his head. "What would you like?"

"Sketti," Mato said, and I looked at John, who rolled his eyes. I guessed there was no spaghetti in the house.

"There's a convenience store on the corner," John told me.

"Do you want to go with me?" I asked Mato, and he nodded vigorously. "I'll walk with him to the store, and we'll be right back." John agreed, and I carried Mato toward the door and out into the evening warmth. "Are you happy to be with your Uncle Akecheta?"

"Yes," Mato answered, still clutching his horse to him as we walked. He didn't say much, but looked all around. As we walked into the store, I took his hand and found a package of spaghetti and a jar of sauce that seemed to meet with Mato's approval, as did the bag of chips and the candy bar I let him get, along with one for his sister. By the time we left, I'd purchased a lot more than spaghetti, but that was fine. Those kids had been through a lot.

We walked back to the apartment, and I held Mato's tiny hand in mine the whole way. Once we reached the apartment, I set down the bag, and Mato rummaged in it for the chocolate bar and then raced to find Ichante. "Those are for after dinner," I called. John came out carrying Ichante, who appeared to have been crying. I cooked dinner as best I could while John spent time with the kids, and after they'd eaten, John put them both to bed while I waited for him on the sofa. He came out of the room very quietly, then closed the door behind him.

"They're asleep," he whispered and collapsed on the sofa next to me. "Once you left, Ichante raced through the apartment opening every door, looking under all the beds, calling for her mother. When she didn't find her, she broke down into sobs and kept asking where she was," John said as he wiped his eyes. "No one explained to Ichante that her mother wasn't coming back, and she kept thinking that once she got to come home with me, her mother would be waiting for her too." John sniffled and looked away.

"I'm sorry, John," I said softly.

"I know she'll be okay, and so will Mato." John turned back to me with tear tracks on his face. "They need to be around family and have some time to heal. I just hope they both learn to trust that nothing is going to happen to them. I know they expect to be taken away again at any time." John wiped his eyes and steadied himself, sitting a bit straighter in the chair. He was going to be all right as well.

I leaned over and gave John a soft kiss. "I'm going to say good night and let you get some rest." I stood up and leaned over, resting my hands on John's knees. "Call me if you need anything, and I'll be right over." I leaned in for a final kiss. "I mean it," I added before heading toward the door. "Call your mother," I said, and John nodded. I saw him reaching for the phone as I left.

The drive home didn't take long, but it gave me time to think. I'd helped John get what he wanted, but I knew those two kids were going to mean a great deal of change for John and for me. I'd gotten used to having John in my life, and in my bed quite a few nights a week, and that was going to change. John wasn't going to be able to stay over, not with the threat of social services hanging over him and the kids. No, chances were that I was going to see him at work and then maybe a few times a week either at the house or at his apartment, but at either place, the intimacy we'd shared would probably be curtailed a great deal. "Careful what you wish for, Jerry," I told myself out loud as I pulled into the driveway. "You may just get it." It wasn't that I begrudged him the kids, because I didn't, at all. They needed John more than anyone else in the world right now, and I understood that, I really did. It was just that I was going to miss him.

I turned off the engine, then walked into the empty house and climbed the stairs. I was worn out, so I cleaned up and fell into bed, placing my cell phone on the nightstand in case John called. It took a while to fall asleep, and I spent a lot of time listening to the house, wishing John were next to me in the bed.

# THE GOOD FIGHT

UNFORTUNATELY, I had to spend a number of nights alone. "Why don't you bring the kids for dinner tonight?" I asked John as we finished work the following Wednesday. "I'd love to see them and you."

"I'd love to see you too," John said as sort of a confession. "I think Mato would, as well. He asks about you. It's Ichante that's worrying me. She seems to be withdrawing from everyone except me and the ladies who watch her. I took her to the grocery store with me, and she stayed close and kept trying to hide behind my legs whenever a white person came close to her. She says she's afraid they'll come and take her away again. I'm really not sure what to do," John told me as he paused at the office door.

"Bring them both over, and maybe we'll arrange for her to have some fun with a white person. It's going to take some time, but we need to help her." My mind was already a bit of a whirl of ideas about what we could do.

John closed the door and walked back to where I was standing. "I should have known you'd try to help. I'm not sure there's much any of us can do, but I'll bring them over for dinner. Just don't be surprised if she spends most of the evening trying to hide from you. She does that with just about everyone." John moved closer and offered a gentle kiss. "We'll be back in about an hour if that's okay."

"Good, I'll see you then," I told John. He hurried out, and as I locked up, I heard his car start and then drive away. Once everything was closed up, I went into the house. There wasn't much to eat, so I hurried to the car and made a quick grocery run before stopping at a toy store and then returning to the house.

I got back just as John was pulling in with the kids. He fussed in the car, getting them out while I carried the food and other things inside. John and the children walked into the kitchen, and Mato hurried to me to be picked up and get a hug. Ichante, as John had described, hid behind his legs, peering at me from around them. "You remember Mr. Jerry. He visited you with me, remember?" John asked, and she nodded slowly. "There's nothing to be afraid of."

"Give her time," I said and began unpacking the groceries in the kitchen. John joined me, with Ichante clinging to him. "That's a very pretty dress," I told her. "Did your uncle get that for you?"

She continued watching me silently, but she did nod slightly. "What are we going to have?" John asked, turning before lifting Ichante into his arms. She clung to him, and my heart ached for her. I knew it wasn't the same thing because I'd been much older, but I knew a bit how she felt. My family had disowned me, and the instant separation had been painful beyond belief. At least I had been old enough to be able to articulate what I was feeling so I could work through it. Ichante didn't have that. She was scared and hurting, and she didn't have the words to express it.

"Chocolate?" Mato asked, pulling at my pant leg. I finished putting away the groceries and closed the refrigerator before lifting him up.

"Maybe. But if I do, you can't have it until after dinner. I did get something you can play with, though," I explained, moving toward the living room. I set Mato on the floor and opened the huge set of building blocks I'd picked up. "You can make anything you want." I turned to Ichante. "You can play too."

I opened the container, and Mato dug right in, dumping out the contents and then sitting on the floor to play. John set Ichante down as well, and she simply stared for the longest time, her hands in her lap. "I'm going to start dinner," I said softly, and John sat on the sofa. I'd just gotten the fixings for hamburgers, and while I put things together, I listened, and after a while I heard what sounded like blocks hitting the wooden floor followed by little boy giggles and laughter. I continued making dinner, peeking into the living room every now and then. John and Mato sat on the floor building towers and knocking them down, while Ichante sat off to the side and watched, clutching the doll John had given her. John must have brought it in the bag of things he'd carried in.

I went back to work, but kept checking. I was about to put on the hamburgers to cook when I peered in one more time. Ichante had moved closer and was building something with the blocks. When Mato knocked it over, she moved away, but then John asked her to help them build the tower, and she moved closer. "Will you be ready to eat soon?" I asked.

"Whenever you are," John told me, and I returned to the kitchen. Cooking didn't take long, and I set everything on the table before calling them to dinner. I didn't have child seats, so I made up a plate for both kids and helped them sit at the table, with a bit of phonebook engineering. John sat with Ichante, and I helped Mato. It was an interesting meal that ended with Mato wearing as much food as he ate and Ichante eating very little. She did eat something, though, and John simply shrugged. We ate as best we could, and I could feel his frustration and concern. After dinner, I split a chocolate bar between the kids, and they both ate that, so things couldn't be too bad.

Cleaning up both of them was interesting, and as soon as Mato was done, he raced back to the blocks. John and Ichante joined him, and once I'd cleaned up, I went into the living room as well. "Can I join you?" I asked, and to my surprise Ichante nodded. I sat down, and we began building a really tall tower. "Who wants to knock this one down?" Mato jumped up and down of course. "I think it's Ichante's turn," I said, and she looked at me before smiling and pushing the very top. The tower toppled with a loud crash and blocks scattered everywhere.

"Can we do it again?" Ichante asked me.

"Of course we can," I told her. "Let's build another one." I knew it was way too soon to be overly pleased, but I felt like I'd won some sort of victory, and we played on the floor with the blocks until both kids began to yawn.

"I think we'd better go," John said, and I nodded, glad they'd come over but disappointed that they were leaving, especially John. I missed him terribly.

It took a while to get the kids' things together. John loaded the car while I sat on the sofa, Mato on one side and Ichante on the other. Mato leaned against me, already half asleep, and Ichante stared up at me a bit skeptically until she too rested her head against me. I swallowed hard, lightly stroking her black hair. When John came into the room, he stopped, and I saw him stare, my own surprise mirrored back to me, mixed with a touch of relief. "I think she likes me," I told John with a smile.

He nodded and quietly stepped closer. "She has good taste," he whispered, and Mato shifted closer, trying to get warm in the cool, air-conditioned room. Ichante moved closer too, and I held them both lightly in my arms. They felt so right, and though I knew they had to leave, that was the last thing I wanted. I kept running through ways I could ask John and the kids to stay. I had room upstairs. There were two bedrooms set up, but they hadn't been used in a while… but no, staying wasn't really a practical option, and I knew it. "I miss you," I finally said, feeling a bit needy, but it was how I felt. I'd only seen John at work for weeks, and I missed spending time with him. Call me selfish, and maybe I was, but I missed having John to myself. I missed his touch and the way he made me feel special when he looked at me. Yes, I was being selfish, and maybe kind of childish, but it was what I wanted.

"I miss you too," John told me as he leaned forward. I braced for him to kiss me, but he lifted Ichante into his arms instead, and a stab of hurt and disappointment jabbed at my heart. I knew, or at least hoped, John still cared for me. "I really do," John added, and I slowly stood up, lifting Mato, and he draped himself on my chest, his small head resting on my shoulder. In that gesture of trust, I could feel him almost steal my heart. Just like their uncle, these kids were worming their way into my heart as well, and I wasn't quite sure how to tell John how I felt.

"I know," I said instead, and I followed John out to the car. I settled Mato in his seat as John got Ichante settled and ready to go. I closed the door as softly as I could and waited as John walked around the car. The heat of the day had dissipated somewhat, but the night was still warm and close feeling. Little light filtered to this part of the drive, so as John reached me, he became cloaked in shadow. As he approached, I stepped closer to him, and John stopped. Without waiting, I slid my arms around his neck and went for a kiss, hard, deep, and as loving as I possibly could give him. John's lips parted, and I slipped my tongue between them, hearing him give me a small moan as I did.

I had to back away because my heart was already racing and my body reacting to John's proximity. I missed him terribly and wanted him so bad, but there was nothing I could do. The kids came first, and that was only right, but it didn't change the way I felt, or the longing that hit me once I ended the kiss and stepped away. "I do miss you, John," I said, and then I realized this could be one of those now-or-never moments. "Aw hell." I grabbed him once again and tugged him into another kiss. "I love you, John," I said, and I felt him hesitate for a second that seemed like a lifetime. "I know we sort of told each other, but I wanted to be plain. I'm in love with you, John, and when you're gone, I miss you terribly. I know you have the kids, and I know that they are the most important thing in your life right now, but I wanted you to know how I felt."

I saw John shake his head in the dimness, and my heart sank. I backed away slightly and turned away so I wouldn't have to see him as he told me what I'd been afraid of.

"I love you too," he said, and I felt him touch my shoulder. "I know things are kind of crazy right now, but that doesn't change the way I feel." I turned around, wishing I could see John's eyes, but all I could see was his outline against the light from the house behind. "The kids need me, and I can't leave them."

"I know," I said, because I did understand. I knew the words from the social worker kept running through John's mind, and he was trying to provide as much care and attention as he could manage. "There are a lot of demands on your time."

"We'll figure something out," he told me, and I saw him reach out and slide his hand over my cheek. "I'd better get them home." John lowered his hand along my arm, taking my hand in his for a second, and then the touch faded away. John opened the car door, the overhead light shining on his face. In that second, he turned to look at me, and I saw how he felt in his eyes. John got in the car and closed the door, and it seemed a bit like he was gone. He started the engine and turned on the headlights. I stepped back, and he backed the car out of the drive, the lights shining on me as I lifted my hand to wave good-bye. Then the lights passed, and I was cast in darkness once again as John's taillights moved away and then disappeared from sight. I slowly walked back into the house, which now felt emptier than it had before.

CHAPTER
# TEN

OVER the next few weeks, John and the kids came for dinner and to spend the evening a few times a week, and on the following Saturday, we took them to the water park, which was a huge hit. I'd asked John if they'd like to stay, but he declined, he did agree that the following Saturday he'd see if the kids were up for a sleepover. All week I'd been looking forward to it and hoping that everything would work out, and on the last Saturday of August, I watched as John drove his old car into my driveway. He helped the kids out, and they ran up the porch, each carrying a sleeping bag in their arms. "We gonna sweep over!" Mato said with glee, bouncing on his little legs.

Ichante was more reserved, but even she looked excited. "Sleep over," she corrected her brother, and then she smiled up at me. The change in her in a few weeks had been remarkable. She still tended to cling to John, but her own personality and assertiveness were beginning to come through. Ichante was still cautious and careful, but she also smiled more. At the water park the previous week, she'd explored, but only went where John was. Mato had been more adventurous, but even he was still a bit tentative.

I led them into the house, with John bringing up the rear, looking a bit like a pack mule. Once we were inside, I helped John set down all the bags, and we showed Mato and Ichante their rooms. "You can sleep here if you like, or Uncle John and I can set up a tent in one of the rooms, and you can sleep there." That got an excited cry and set Mato to jumping up and down, while Ichante simply looked at John. "Or I can set up the tent for Mato, and Ichante can have her own room," I amended, and I showed her where she could sleep.

"It's pretty," Ichante said as she stepped into the room.

"My grandmother decorated this room for herself," I told Ichante as she set her sleeping bag on the bed. Grandma had set up this room years ago as her sewing room, and after she died, Grandpa had kept it just the same. The flowered wallpaper was a bit faded, but the lounge chair in the corner was comfortable, and the bedspread was covered in flowers as well. I'd sort of hoped that Ichante would like the room. Mato burst into the room, chattering up a storm. I couldn't understand a word, but he was obviously excited. Taking his hand, I let him lead me back to his room, and he showed me a box he'd found at the end of the bed.

"Those are some of the toys I had when I was your age," I explained, and Mato stared into what probably looked like a treasure chest to him. "You can play with them if you want." When I'd come to live with Grandpa, I'd found that many of the things they'd bought for me when I was a child were still here. "My grandma and grandpa bought me those when I was a kid," I said as I helped Mato lift one of the trucks out of the toy box. He looked at it almost reverently before dropping down and running it over the floor, making engine noises. I reached into the box and found a small stuffed dog and brought it to Ichante, who smiled as she took it. "Let's go back downstairs and we'll make lunch." I held out my hand, and Ichante took it. Mato was more interested in the truck, but followed, rolling it along the hallway and then along each step as he went down.

In the kitchen, John slipped his arm around my waist as I worked to make sandwiches. "It looks like everything's okay," John commented, looking through the dining room to the living room, where the kids played on the floor.

"They're kids who've been through a lot, but they're resilient and they feel safe now. Ichante even spoke to me."

"She's always been quiet, but she's talking more and starting to ask questions about what is going to happen to her and Mato. I've explained that their mother isn't coming back and that they are going to live with me from now on." I saw a hard look flash across John's face, and I knew the ugly white woman would have a battle on her hands if she tried anything, but he didn't say anything about her, and I couldn't blame him. "She still asks about her mother, and I try to tell her stories about when we were kids. Mato hasn't asked, but I suspect he might in time, although he was awfully young when she passed."

"Hey," I whispered, angling my face toward John, "I'm glad you're here." John tightened his arms around me, angling his face for a light kiss. The brief taste begged for more, and I set the knife I was using on the counter, turning in his arms before going in for a deeper kiss. It had been too long since I'd had John to myself for more than a few minutes, and I was determined to make the most of it. I knew we could only kiss, but I had every intention of making this the best kiss ever, and from the soft groan that echoed in John's throat, I'd say I succeeded. John tugged me closer, and I got tactile confirmation as John's hips pressed to mine. God, I wanted him so bad, and my mind began working through scenarios where I could get him upstairs. Of course that wasn't practical, but my lust-addled, sex-deprived brain was getting a bit desperate.

"Once the kids are asleep," John whispered between pants when he broke the kiss. "I promise." I nodded and returned to making lunch, anything to keep my mind off John's scent and the way he looked in those tight jeans. John worked with me, and I did my best to concentrate on the task rather than him.

"Come to the table," I called through the house as I carried the plate of sandwiches to the dining area. John had brought booster seats, and he helped the kids into their places as I brought drinks and chips to the table. Mato began eating right away, getting as much food on his face as he did in his belly. Ichante was more careful, but she too tended to leave a trail of crumbs around her. "Should we clean them up?" I asked halfway through the meal.

"We may as well wait until they're done," John answered with a grin, although he did wipe both their hands. We ate, sharing the occasional smile as we both kept an eye on the kids. When they were done, we led them to the bathroom to clean up, and then they played on the living room floor with their toys while John and I finished eating. The whole scene was blissfully domestic, and I never thought it would make me as happy as it did.

"Can we go outside?" Mato asked as we began to clear the table, carrying his truck along with him.

"Sure. Once we're done, you and Ichante can play on the porch," I told him, and he hurried away on his hands and knees, scooting the truck along the floor. "They really are something else," I said to John as we carried the dishes into the kitchen.

"Aren't they?" John commented with a proud smile, and I had to agree.

"I have Popsicles and ice cream for later," I told John, showing him where they were. "I'll also make up some lemonade for when we sit on the porch."

Once we'd cleaned up and I'd made the lemonade, John and I herded the kids outside and then sat on the porch as they raced around the yard. "We need to get them bicycles. Ichante is probably old enough for one with training wheels, and Mato could certainly have a tricycle. There's enough room for them to ride along the sidewalk and up the drive if we moved the cars to the street."

"We?" John asked, catching my particular pronoun.

"Yes, we," I emphasized, and he moved a little closer.

"I'm not quite sure what we would do without you," John said as he watched the kids play. "If it weren't for you, they'd still be at the mercy of the ugly white woman."

"Have you heard from her since she dropped off the kids?" I asked, and John shook his head.

"I did get a letter from her stating that each of the kids should have their own bedroom, but there's no way I can afford a bigger place right now. Since then, there hasn't been anything at all. I think she realizes that we mean business, and they want this whole lawsuit to go away," John said. "The state is contesting our ability to actually charge them with kidnapping, and the courts are weighing that right now. The lawyer says it's slow, but the tribe seems determined to pursue this to the end. Not just for Mato and Ichante, but for all our children. He says the state has abused its authority and it's time someone took them to task."

"Can the tribe afford it?"

John smiled. "The lawyer is a tribe member, and he's doing this for free, but we take care of our own, and the tribe will see that he's rewarded in some way."

"You know, I'm sort of jealous of that." I reached to the pitcher of lemonade and poured a glass for myself and John. The kids heard the ice tinkling, and they bounded up the steps, so I poured small glasses for them too. They drank in a hurry and then raced back into the yard. I had no idea what they were playing, but it seemed to make sense to them. "You have a whole group of people who have your back without thinking about it. The people

151

who should be like that for me turned away." The old hurt began to surface once again. No matter how hard I tried to keep it at bay, the ache bubbled up every now and then.

"I'm pretty lucky to have a mother like Kiya. She may not fully understand, but she'll fight like a mountain lion for any of her kids. Her name means 'to fly', but she should really be Zuya, warrior woman, because that's what she is."

"What does your name mean?" All this time, and I'd just realized I'd never asked.

"Warrior," John answered and looked to the kids. "Mato means 'bear' and Ichante is 'from the heart'. We name our children based upon what we want for them, and it's sometimes amazing how close we come and sometimes how very far away."

I let my gaze shift to the children. "I can see a bear in Mato; he's strong and protective. Ichante is sweet and takes things to heart easily. They seem incredibly appropriately named."

"I wasn't talking about them," John explained, and I shifted on the swing, my feet stopping its movement.

"If you're talking about yourself, then I think you're wrong. You're perfectly named." John widened his eyes in surprise. "A warrior runs toward the gunfire, no matter how much he wants to protect himself and head the other way. You do that. You battled for those kids for months. You and your tribe are taking on the entire state. Not all battles are fought with guns or fists; some are fought with words and by standing up for what's right and what's yours. You do that all the time." I watched as Mato raced around his sister as she sat on the grass. "And in this case, those two were the reward."

"But you helped," John said.

"Warriors don't always go it alone," I told him, and John turned away. "And they don't always win, but they persist and give it everything they have."

"You should have been a warrior," he told me, and I shifted so I could lean close.

"I'll settle for being the warrior's lover," I whispered, and saw John leer back at me.

"Keep those kids off my lawn!"

I turned and saw Old Man Hooper glaring at Mato as he raced back to the yard, carrying his truck.

"They're only kids and won't hurt anything," I called back as nicely as I could. How Grandpa put up with the old coot all those years was beyond me. The way he carried on, you'd think his lawn was a manicured masterpiece rather than mowed weeds. I'd taken to spreading weed killer farther and farther into his yard to stop the spread of his crap into mine.

"I don't want them on my property," Mr. Hooper shot back with a glare, and Mato stared up at me. Ichante tried to hide behind the tree in the front yard.

"Scaring small children now?" I called as I stood up. "You should feel like a real man now that you've terrified a three-year-old." I stared at him across the divide between our porches, and he went back inside. I motioned Mato over. "If your toy goes on his yard, just tell me and I'll get it for you."

"Are you gonna beat him up?" Mato asked, and I laughed.

"Nah," I told him. "I wouldn't want to get old grump cooties." I shuddered a little, and Mato fell on the ground laughing as he sort of sang "old grump cooties" over and over. The excitement faded, and the kids returned to their playing.

"He's going to cause trouble," John warned, and I looked at Mr. Hooper's empty porch.

"He was a grouch when I was a kid. He's just an unhappy, lonely old codger. Grandpa used to be friends with him, but that was a long time ago. They had some sort of falling out after

Grandma died. I don't know what it was over, though. Probably never will, because I'm certainly not going to ask him." I turned to where the kids were playing. "Who wants a Popsicle?"

I got a chorus of "I do's," including one from John, and I went inside and returned with four of them. They were actually fruit pops of some sort, and we all settled in the shade, sucking on the frozen treats. I brought paper towels for both kids, and they needed them as juice began running down their arms. They didn't care, and I only tried to keep the worst of it off their clothes. Not that it really succeeded, but they had fun and that was what counted.

John's phone rang and I heard him talking to what sounded like another parent. "I'm at a friend's," John explained before listening and then turning to me. "One of Ichante's friends, Macy, wants to know if she can play."

"If her mom wants to bring Macy over, that would be fine," I told John, and he relayed the message before providing directions. Then he hung up and shoved the phone back in his pocket.

"Thanks," John said. "Macy's the first friend Ichante's made, and the girls seem to have really connected." John began cleaning up the kids as they finished their treats. "Macy's mom is bringing her over, so I want you both to go inside and wash up." John helped Ichante, and I led Mato to the kitchen sink, where I cleaned his hands and face. As soon as we were done, he raced through the house and back outside to play with his truck. I joined him after getting a car from the toy box and then waited on the porch for John and Ichante to join us.

The kids played quietly on their own until a minivan pulled into the drive. A young girl got out, and she and Ichante greeted each other with hugs before they both carried their dolls under the shade of the tree. A young woman stepped up onto the porch, and I stood as John introduced her as Elizabeth. "Please have a seat.

Would you like some lemonade?" I asked, and I poured her a glass when she accepted.

"Thank you for letting Macy come over," Elizabeth said. "She's done nothing but talk about playing with Ichante all day."

"It's no problem," John answered, and I nodded. Mato had joined the girls, and all three of them were playing quietly while the three of us talked.

"You were on the news again last night," Elizabeth told John, and he nodded. "I think it's terrible what they're doing," she went on to say. "They said the governor is calling for an investigation. Who knows if anything will come of it, but at least it's out in the open now." Elizabeth took a drink from her glass. She was a small, thin woman with short black hair and neatly pressed clothes.

"Yes, it is. Maybe what happened to Mato and Ichante won't happen to other children," John said rather sternly. I noticed our crotchety neighbor had come out on his porch and sat down to watch the kids so they didn't trample his weeds.

"Do you have children?" Elizabeth asked.

"No. I've never been married," I answered, looking at John for some sort of sign as to what Elizabeth knew.

"They're fags!" came the cry across the lawn, and all three of us turned to stare at the opposite porch. "I saw them kissing the other night. Shouldn't be around children at all."

Elizabeth looked at John, and then me, and I was preparing for her to get up and take Macy and go home, but she simply sat back in her chair, turning toward Mr. Hooper. "Please—where have you been for the last century?" she fired back at him, shaking her head. "You know, you really should just keep your ignorance to yourself." I raised my glass and tinked it against the side of hers.

155

"Here, here," I said before taking a drink. "Would you and Macy like to stay for dinner?"

She accepted, and we spent much of the rest of the afternoon talking and watching the kids play. Mato got cranky, and when I settled him in on the love seat with a pillow and his truck, he fell asleep five minutes later. The girls continued playing together for hours.

Macy and Elizabeth stayed for a light dinner, and then Elizabeth bundled Macy home while John got the kids ready for bed. Once they were set, I said good night to both of them and got a hug from each of them, the one from Ichante a bit of a welcome surprise. Mato, of course, insisted on sleeping in the tent for about five minutes, and then asked to have his sleeping bag moved to the bed. Once they were all set, we said good night and quietly descended the stairs.

"They're amazing kids," I told John as we sat in front of the television, the volume low so we could hear if they got up or needed anything. After about half an hour, John checked on them and reported that both of them were sound asleep. "Then let's go up to bed ourselves," I suggested before getting up and starting to turn off the lights. We climbed the stairs quietly, and John made a final check on the kids before joining me in my room.

"Damn," John whispered when he came in, closing the door behind him. I lay on the bed wearing only my underwear, showing off a very pronounced bulge. John tugged off his shirt and prowled closer. He kicked off his shoes, and I heard them slide along the floor. Then John opened his pants, slipping them down his legs, and he stood near the bed in all his naked glory.

"Damn, yourself," I countered as John climbed onto the bed. Our mouths found each other's, and John stroked lightly along my chest as his kisses became deeper and more demanding. I tugged John on top of me, hissing slightly as his skin met mine. It had been so long since I'd felt him like this. I was instantly hard,

156

and I ran my hands down John's back to his butt, grasping the firm globes in my hands. "God, you feel good," I told him, and John mumbled something before licking his way down my neck to work his lips at my shoulder. "Yes," I hissed, tightening my grip on his ass.

"What do you want?" he asked against my skin, sending a shiver through me when he blew over dampened areas.

"Fuck me, John," I told him. "I want to feel you again." I wasn't in the mood for soft and slow. I wanted him, and I wanted him right now. I slid my briefs down my hips, and John pushed them the rest of the way off my legs. As soon as the fabric was gone, I wrapped my legs around John's waist, kissing him hard as I silently begged for what I wanted. John caressed down my sides and over my butt, ghosting his fingers over my entrance. As soon as I felt his featherlight touch on my sensitive skin, I sucked harder on his lips, driving my tongue into his mouth the way I wanted to feel him deep inside me.

"I will," John whispered against my lips. "But only once I've gotten you good and ready." John shifted off me, and in a flash he had me rolled onto my stomach and was sliding down me. He pressed my legs apart, caressing along the inside of my thigh. "I want to see you throb for me," John muttered, lightly tapping his fingers on my opening. I arched my back, willing him to press inside, but he didn't. He rubbed his fingers and teased my flesh until I had to bite my lips to keep from crying out. Then he stopped and the bed shifted. John spread my cheeks, and I knew what was coming next. Even so, I still moaned as John probed me with his tongue, thrusting inside me as my muscles spasmed and throbbed around him.

"John," I groaned, grabbing handfuls of bedding in my fists. I buried my head in the pillow, making all kinds of needy sounds that filled my head and were swallowed by the pillow rather than filling the room. I'd nearly forgotten the way John could play my body like a fine instrument. Every nerve in my body sang as he worked me higher and higher with his tongue. John lifted my hips, and I slid my knees under me, ass in the air as he continued rimming me to oblivion and stroking along my length until I could barely think straight.

Everything stopped, the licking, the touches, and the bed went totally still. I lifted my head away from the pillow and heard a package rip open followed by the snick of a bottle. I lowered my hips back onto the bed and waited. John pressed to my opening and held still, his weight settling on top of me, lips nipping at my ear. Then he pressed inside me, and I stretched to accommodate him. The burn hurt some at first, and I swallowed the cry that threatened as the pain shifted quickly to pleasure. John sank deeper and deeper into me, filling me perfectly, until I felt his hips against my cheeks. Then he stilled and I caught my breath. "You have to be quiet," John told me, and I nodded.

Slowly John began to withdraw, and I held my breath. John completely pulled out and then slid deep back into me. I gasped as quietly as I could, the searing pleasure reaching to the tips of my fingers and toes. My entire body tingled as John rocked back and forth above me, dragging his cock over the spot inside me. "I love you," John whispered into my ear as he snapped his hips. I arched my back and had to swallow my cry before it crossed my lips. John thrust deep and stopped, his cock throbbing inside me. "You're an amazing man, and I love you more than I can say."

My head throbbed as I heard those words. I opened my mouth to say something to John, and he pulled back, then drove deep once again. All tangible thought flew from my head, and I began to float. I swore I'd rise to the ceiling if John weren't holding me down. "I love you too," I gasped as pressure built from deep inside. My head got light, and I could feel the blood rushing through me as my entire body became hypersensitive to everything around me. Clamping my eyes closed, I felt my release hang just out of reach, and then John drove deep, and I plummeted off the summit, flying through the air as I came.

I felt John coming as well as he joined me in flight. Slowly, we returned to earth, with John holding me, his warm breath caressing the back of my neck. "Am I hurting you?" John asked, and I shook my head, not wanting him to move a muscle. After a few minutes, John shifted slowly, our bodies separating with mutual groans. I immediately missed him, and I heard John pad across the floor and carefully crack the door open. He left and then returned in a few seconds with a towel. We cleaned up quickly and then pulled on clean underwear before climbing back under the covers. We kissed, and John held me tight as we fell asleep together.

During the night I woke to an empty bed and fumbled around for my robe before padding down the hall. I saw John come out of Mato's room. "Is everything okay?" I whispered, and John nodded, walking back to my bedroom.

"I just wanted to check on them," John explained once the door was closed. He slipped out of the robe and got back into bed. "Sometimes they have nightmares, and I need to be there to soothe them, but they're both sleeping like angels." John seemed relieved, and we easily fell back to sleep.

I woke hours later to the doorbell. Jumping out of bed, I grabbed my robe and hurried down the stairs. "Shhh," I said as I opened the door, stopping in my tracks as the ugly white woman stood on my porch, looking as severe as usual. "The kids are sleeping," I told her through the screen door.

"So they *are* here," she said as though it were an accusation.

"Yeah, so?" I countered, folding my arms across my chest, staring at her through the door. I heard John come up behind me.

"We got a call from a neighbor that the kids were in an unhealthy environment," she said and reached for the door. I beat her to it and threw the lock.

"You aren't welcome here, and unless you have a court order, you are not entering this house."

"I don't need one. Those children were placed in his probationary care that we can revoke anytime we wish. Now open the door, or I'll have to call the police."

"No, they're not," John said from behind me. "I have already filed to adopt the children, and my attorney brought up their past treatment at the hands of your agency." John moved away, and I followed him with my eyes before turning back to her. We traded glares through the door until John returned. "I have been granted temporary custody of both Mato and Ichante pending finalization of the adoption. The order also states that the court will make a final decision based upon a review of my home independent of child services." John held the order to the door. "It seems the judge seemed to think the case of kidnapping against the state has merit. So call the police—we'll have you arrested."

Her demeanor changed instantly. Gone was the accusatory stare, and for the first time, I saw a touch of fear in her eyes. "I'm just doing my job, and we did get a call."

"Who made it?" I asked.

"The call was to our anonymous tip line, but we need to investigate each of them."

"So based on an anonymous tip from a man who was probably a complete lunatic, you were ready to traumatize these children again." I stepped forward, standing right in front of the door. "John's kids have been through hell. It's taken weeks to get Ichante so she isn't afraid of her own shadow, and on the basis of a crank call, you were ready to pull them away from their family rather than find out exactly what was happening. If that's how you operate, you deserve to go to jail." I reached for the door to close it.

"I have to see the kids," she explained, and I stopped, looking at John, who nodded.

"Fine, but if you upset them in any way, I'll call the police. And if you think for a minute I won't find something to charge you with, you've got another think coming." I unlocked the door and stepped back, letting her open it and step inside.

"The children are sleeping upstairs," John said, and he quietly led the way. I followed, and John opened the guest room door. Mato was just waking up, and John soothed him, lifting him out of the bed, and he immediately rested his head on John's shoulder.

"I'll take him," I said, and Mato went right to me, still half asleep. I held him, rubbing Mato's back, and John opened Ichante's door. I heard him call her lightly, and he stepped into the room. "Just wait here," I told the social worker, but she wouldn't listen and walked into the room. All I heard was a squeal followed by a scream and then tears. I set Mato down and reached into the room, taking the social worker by the arm and pulling her out as she sputtered and fought me. "That is because of you!" I told her harshly, and she stopped moving, staring at me. I motioned for her to wait and told Mato to go back to bed. He wiped his eyes and walked to his room. "I'll be there in a minute." Once his door closed, I turned back to the social worker.

"She was screaming," the social worker said, trying to head back into the room.

"That little girl is so traumatized by you and your department that just seeing you was enough to upset her. She thinks you're going to take her away, and I'll be damned if I'm going to let that happen. Now, I suggest you get out of this house before I throw you out by your ears. The children were fine until they saw you, and you better believe that I'm going to be on the phone to the director of the agency in Pierre tomorrow morning and talking to reporters tonight."

"I'm just trying to do my job," she explained as I followed her down the stairs.

"Yeah. The Nazis tried to use that same excuse. I'm not buying it, lady. If someone from your agency wishes to meet with the kids, they can call and make arrangements, because I'm also calling the lawyer, and we'll make sure the judge hears about this as well." I kept it up all the way to the front door. By the time I opened it, she looked about as beaten down as I'd ever seen anyone.

"I don't make the rules," she told me lamely.

"Bullshit. Your agency makes its own rules and then changes them to benefit themselves. I've been online and I've seen story after story about children like Mato and Ichante. Other states don't have this issue, only ours, and I intend to see that things change. And if that means some heads roll and people end up on unemployment, so be it. Have a good morning, because I can guarantee tomorrow won't be one." She left the house, and I closed the door behind her and locked it. Then I hurried upstairs.

I found Mato in his sister's room, John trying to calm them both. "She's gone and she's not coming back," I told all three of them.

"She's not gonna take me?" Ichante asked, and I shook my head.

"No one is going to take you away from your Uncle Akecheta." Ichante wiped her eyes and looked at both of us. "Your uncle will fight for you with everything he has." Both kids hugged their uncle at the same time, and I left the room to get dressed and make some breakfast.

As I was working in the kitchen, I heard doors open and close upstairs and then what could only be John's footsteps on the stairs, with a couple of giggle monsters in tow. It was great to hear them laugh.

John got the kids set in their places at the table, and I brought a basic breakfast to the table. Ichante seemed more animated than usual, and I think maybe she was finally realizing that she was safe. Mato chattered as he ate, and both kids laughed as John made faces at them.

Once breakfast was over, John took the kids upstairs to get them cleaned up and dressed while I cleaned up the dishes. When they all came back down, the kids played in the living room and John found me in the kitchen, finishing the last of the dishes. "I got a call from a man at child services, and he said he needs to see the kids this morning." I immediately tensed, and John continued. "He said that they do need to take each complaint seriously and that all he's going to do is make sure the anonymous report they received is truly false. I explained about the ugly white woman, and he told me that she will not be coming." John seemed nervous as he whispered.

"I know you're worried, and maybe it's time you told your story. That reporter who contacted you after the lawsuit was filed—maybe it's time to call her," I suggested, and John looked skeptical but seemed to think about it for a minute before nodding slightly.

"Maybe she can help," John admitted halfheartedly. "Will you call her?" John fished out his wallet and found the card before handing it to me. He joined the kids, and I found my phone, then dialed the number on the card. To my surprise, she answered. "Tonya Smithson."

"This is Jerry Lincoln, and I'm calling on behalf of John Black Raven. Are you still interested in talking to him?" I could hear her moving around.

"Very much. His story sounds fascinating, and we'd love to do a feature about him," She sounded excited, and I could almost imagine her already reaching for a notebook. "Would it be okay if I bring a photographer so I can get a few pictures of him with the kids?"

"I don't see why not. Someone from child services is on their way over, and we expect them in a few minutes...." I left the rest unsaid, and I could already hear what sounded like rushing footsteps.

"We'll be right over. Can I have the address?" she asked. I gave her my home address. "Thank you!" she added exuberantly before hanging up. I disconnected the call and found John in the living room with the kids.

"It's going to be a busy day," I told him with a smile. "She's on her way now."

"Who?" Ichante asked a little fearfully.

"A nice lady who wants to talk to you so she can put you in the newspaper and even take your picture," I told her, and she seemed happy.

"No ugly white woman?" she asked.

"Nope," John told her, and she went back to playing.

"We really need to stop calling her that," I told John with a grin, and he nodded with an evil leer.

"We probably should, but we won't." John laughed, and I kissed him quickly. "Is there anything we should do when the reporter gets here?"

"No. Just be yourself and tell her exactly what's happened. She wants to do a feature, and there's plenty of drama in the story, so just be honest and let your sincerity come through. I doubt she's out to try to make you look bad, and I'll be here with you." I wondered if we should be doing this at John's apartment rather than here, but maybe a more neutral location for John was best. I really wasn't sure, but he seemed okay with doing it here, and I wasn't going to rock the boat.

A soft rap on the door pulled me out of my thoughts, and I went to answer it, seeing a small man standing on the porch with a messenger bag over his shoulder. "Can I help you?"

"I'm Steven Dobbs from child services. I called this morning," he said pleasantly. "I'm looking for John Black Raven."

"Jerry Lincoln, a friend of John's," I said, and I opened the door.

John joined me at the door. "I want to stress that I'm only here to speak with the children," Steven said as laughter drifted in from the other room. "It sounds like they're having fun."

"We do have a court order," John began, and Steven put up his hand.

"I'm not here to take the children, and I'm well aware of my colleague's...." He paused. "... overzealous behavior. I'm simply here to make sure there is no validity to the report we received." John stepped back skeptically and led the way into the living room, where the kids were playing with the blocks. "Hello," Steven said pleasantly, and both kids looked up at him. Ichante stiffened slightly and looked to John.

"It's okay," John said, and she returned to playing. I don't know what I had been expecting, but it wasn't for Steven to pull off his messenger bag and sit on the floor with them. He told them his name and asked for theirs. The kids seemed to accept him almost right away, and soon they were building towers together, with the kids taking turns knocking them over. He asked questions and the kids seemed to open up, with Ichante telling him most of her life story. After about half an hour, Steven said good-bye to the kids and picked up his bag once again.

"These kids are remarkably happy given everything they've been through. I read their case file before I came over and—" Steven cut himself off, shaking his head. "I can't say anything more." He really didn't need to. His eyes said everything. "I understand you've petitioned for adoption," Steven added, and John nodded, still looking a bit like he was waiting for the other shoe to drop. "That's wonderful. I'm going to request that I be added as Mato and Ichante's caseworker, at least until the adoption is finalized."

"Thank you," John said, and I could hear the relief in his voice. We walked him to the door. John said good-bye and joined the children while I stepped outside.

"Thank you," I told Steven and watched as he descended the steps. As I was about to go back inside, I saw Mr. Hooper sitting on his porch.

"It was you, wasn't it? You called child services," I accused.

"So what if I did? Perverts shouldn't be taking care of children," Mr. Hooper shot back self-righteously.

Steven had been about to get into his car, but I saw him stop. "I'm with child services. Were you the one who placed a call yesterday?" Mr. Hooper suddenly seemed a little less confident. "Because making false calls is illegal and can result in your prosecution."

"They're perverts," Mr. Hooper countered. "In my day—"

"I'll have you know that I happen to be gay, and I don't appreciate your sentiments. You don't get to decide who can and can't raise children." Steven stepped toward Mr. Hooper's front steps. "I could very well call the police and have you arrested for making a false report." Steven glared at Mr. Hooper, and he eventually humphed and went inside. I watched as Steven walked back to his car and waved before pulling away. As he left, a truck pulled up and what I suspected was the reporter and her photographer came up the walk. As I'd said, it was going to be quite a day.

THE kids were exhausted, and once we fed them their lunch, they both fell asleep on the sofa. The reporter had left after talking with John and the kids for nearly an hour and a half, and the house was nearly silent. "Do you think it's finally over?" John asked, and I nodded, pulling him into my arms.

"I think so. Now all you need to do is wait for the adoption to be finalized in a few months."

"I know. It's just been a long battle, and I'm tired of fighting. The kids are healthy and seem so much happier than they were. My mother wants to see them, and I thought that next weekend I'd take them over for a visit," John said, and I felt a stab of disappointment.

"I understand," I said, releasing John from the hug and slowly moving away. "The kids have to come first." I'd been afraid of this for a while, and I knew I should have seen it coming. John moved closer and I backed away. "I do understand, I really do."

"No, you don't, Jerry. I want you to come with us. It wouldn't be the same for them or for me without you. I love you, Jerry, and I want to be with you as much as I can. I know the kids make it hard, but...." John swallowed. "You're the person I want to share my life with and the one I want to help raise Mato and Ichante." John hugged me close. "I love you more than anything, and if I don't say it often enough, I'm saying it now. I love you, Jerry Lincoln."

"And I love you, Akecheta Black Raven." John kissed me hard, and I felt my knees go weak. I knew we couldn't do anything with the kids in the next room, but just knowing how

John felt was enough to have me floating on cloud nine. "I have a question for you," I said once John slipped his lips away from mine. "After the adoption is finalized, will you and the kids move in here with me?" Instead of happy, John looked conflicted. "What is it?"

"I want Ichante and Mato to know my people's ways, and I was going to ask you to move with us to the reservation. I want the kids to know their heritage, and I want to figure out a way to teach what I've learned and help my people somehow lift themselves out of the quagmire they're in." John stopped rambling, and I stared at him, fearing where he was going with this. "But that isn't practical. Your business is here, and I can't ask Bryce to move too."

A stab of fear shot to my gut. Was John leaving? After what he'd just said to me, it didn't make sense. "What are you saying?"

"I don't know." John lifted his gaze to look into my eyes. "I mean, yes. I would be happy to make my home here with you. I don't know what I was thinking. You're here, and my life is here with you."

"John, if you'd rather—" I began, and he cut me off with a hard kiss that lasted until the crash of blocks broke the mood. Mato was awake.

"I was being ridiculous. I'd like to return to the reservation so I could help my people, but there's nothing there for Mato and Ichante. They would be with people like them, yes, but here they can have a chance at a better life."

"I've been giving that some thought ever since we had dinner at your mother's. Actually it was your cousin who gave me the idea." I was about to tell John about it when Mato called us into the living room. He and Ichante had built a tower taller than they were. At first, I wondered how they'd managed this feat, and then I saw shoe prints on the coffee table. "You little scamp," I called as I scooped Mato up, his giggles filling the room.

"I told him he was being naughty," Ichante said just before John grabbed her, flying her around the room. As soon as I set Mato back on his feet, he pushed the tower over and it fell to the floor with a crash. He jumped up and down with excitement and then began building again. John and I sat on the sofa, watching the kids play with smiles on our faces.

"So what's this big idea of yours?" John asked.

# CHAPTER
# ELEVEN

WE DIDN'T get to the reservation the following weekend. In fact, we weren't able to go for almost a month. Kiya did manage to come for a visit, though, and she spent the weekend with her grandchildren. John, Bryce, and I spent those weeks working like crazy, and it wasn't until mid-September that we were able to get far enough ahead to be able to take an entire weekend off. The adoption seemed to be proceeding according to plan, and with any luck the final papers would be signed by Halloween. We'd left Friday right after work and had driven well into the night, arriving at John's mother's house just before midnight. The kids were both asleep in their seats and had stopped asking if we were there yet a few hours ago.

We got them unpacked and into bed with a minimum of fuss—thankfully John had thought to get the kids into their pajamas early—and then joined Kiya in the living room after placing our bags in the room she'd designated for us. "So what's this big idea you want my help with?" Kiya asked me after I'd barely had a chance to sit down.

"Mom, we just drove all this way. Can't it wait until tomorrow?" John asked with a yawn, but even I knew the answer to that.

"I'll do better than that," I told her, and I went out to the car, popped open the trunk, and pulled out a box that I'd brought along. I took it into the house, set it on the living room floor, and then pulled out a laptop computer and handed it to Kiya. "I have eight of these in the box. They're all a few years old, but John and I made sure they work and have some basic software on them. I was wondering if you'd be willing to arrange to find eight families with kids that could use them. I have more of them at home, but these were all I could bring with all the other stuff."

"I don't understand," Kiya said, turning the laptop in her hand.

"John told me that many of the people on the reservation are struggling, and I thought that if I could put a computer into the hands of some children who wouldn't get one otherwise, then maybe they could learn how to use it, and we might open doors for them." I was a computer guy, and so was John. So I'd thought that maybe some of the reservation kids would have the chance to find out what their talents were. "There's an old saying about giving a man a fish and he'll eat for a day; teach him to fish, and he'll feed himself for a lifetime. These computers can help teach the children to fish." I hoped I'd gotten my point across, but I wasn't really sure.

"Mom, think about it. There are lots of families with smart kids at the school who could use a computer. We could give them one to help them learn. Like Jerry said, we have more and we could send them to you. You could give them to the teachers too, if they needed them."

"But eight is such a small number," Kiya said. "We need so many more."

"We can send more," I told her. "I have clients who are willing to donate used equipment. That's where I got these. The problem is that I'm not a charity, and I was hoping you might know of a group who could act as the umbrella charity so my clients could deduct what they donate." I'd talked to my lawyer, and setting up the charity was possible, but it would take some work.

"I think I know just the thing," she said. "The school itself is a nonprofit, and donations to it are charitable. Let me talk to the principal, and I'll get back to you. Maybe we can work this out." She sounded excited, and as I took back the computer and placed it in the box, her expression became serious, and I wondered what was on her mind. Glancing at John, I could see the same confusion on his face. "Why are you doing this?" Kiya asked seriously. "Not that I'm ungrateful, but you've known my son for about four months, and you offer him a job, help him get custody of the children, and now you offer to help the children on the reservation."

"Mom!" John snapped a little harshly. "I wouldn't think you'd look a gift horse in the mouth."

"We have to, you know that," she said, not rising to John's anger, and then she settled her gaze on me.

My stomach squirmed, because I'd never really thought why I was doing these things—I just was. "It may sound like some sort of romantic notion, because it sort of does to me too, but I want John's family to be my family. He's the other half of me, sometimes the better half." I gazed at John and smiled, taking his hand. "I have no family of my own. They turned their back on me years ago, but I love your son." I squeezed John's hand and felt him squeeze mine in return. "I don't blame you for being suspicious, just like the council was when I spoke with them, but Akecheta knows what's in my heart, just like I know his."

172

Kiya's gaze raked over both of us, and I felt like squirming but forced myself to return it and wait her out. I expected her to say something, but all she did was nod with a slight smile on her face and then stand up to leave the room.

"Let's go to bed," John said, and I followed him down the hall. We checked on the kids, who were sound asleep, before going to the bedroom and closing the door behind us.

I sat down on the side of the bed, watching John as he opened our suitcase. "Why do I get the feeling all that was some sort of test?"

"It probably was. Mom's always been protective, and with Dad gone so much, she's gotten even more so," John explained as he pulled off his shirt, the bedside light glistening off his richly colored skin. I watched as he finished undressing and climbed onto the bed.

"I wish I knew if I'd passed," I said, turning to look at John.

"Oh, you did," John said, kissing and licking the base of my neck. "You definitely did," he added as he tugged me back onto the mattress. I fell willingly, my head resting in John's lap. Looking up at him, I wondered just what he had in mind as my ears brushed the warm skin of his legs. I loved touching him any way I could, and my eyes drifted closed as I felt John's fingers stroke my temples. "You're an amazing man, Jerry Lincoln," John told me, and I hummed something as John touched a spot just behind my ear that sent a zing through me. It was sort of like scratching a dog's back and making his leg shake, only instead of making things shake, it made them hard. When I felt John stop, I opened my eyes as he leaned over me, his chest filling my vision.

John began working the buttons of my shirt, touching and caressing my skin as he worked. I couldn't help holding my breath, wondering just how far John was going to go. "We're at your mother's," I moaned softly when my shirt parted and John stroked up and down my chest, then stopped to tease the skin just

173

above my belt. I wanted him so badly. It took all my control to keep from leaping up and pinning John to the bed while I had my way with him. About the only thing that kept me still was John's touch. "Please," I begged, and I heard him chuckle softly.

"We're at my mother's," he teased, stretching so his hands reached just under my belt, and I thrust my hips up for just that little bit more sensation. "We need to be quiet," John added as he cradled my head in his hands and brought our mouths together. I shifted to get a better angle, and we kissed hard and long. "Let's get you out of these clothes."

I mumbled my agreement and began fumbling with my belt buckle. There was no graceful way to do that, so I slid off the bed, shrugging out of my shirt and tugging off my pants as John watched. "What about the kids?" I asked as I rejoined him on the bed and was immediately engulfed in his arms.

"They're so tired, they'll sleep all night long, and if they make a sound, my mother will be there in two seconds. She's been dying to spend time with them, just like I've been looking forward to having you all to myself for a few hours." John kissed me and then pressed me against the mattress. "You're lovely, you know that?" John asked me just before he closed his mouth around one of my nipples.

"No, I'm not," I whined softly. "You're the handsome one," I added, running my fingers through his silky long black hair as the tips of it tickled my skin. I'd never been anything to really look at.

John stilled. "You're lovely to me," he argued playfully even as he stretched my arms over my head. I tried to squirm, but John simply smiled before running his tongue along my side. "Beauty is in the eye of the beholder, and it's what's on the inside that counts."

I chuckled and squirmed as John tickled his way all the way down to my hip. "So you'd say I was beautiful if I looked like

Quasimodo?" I teased, and John chuckled as he licked the spot right at the base of my hip. I thought my eyes would cross forever.

"You talk too much," John said as he licked his way back up my body, "especially when we're in a quiet room with no one to bother us." John licked the other nipple and then moved his tongue in a blazing trail up my neck to my mouth. He had a point, and I shut up and put my lips to much better use. John's weight felt divine, and I kept my hands where he'd put them for no other reason than he seemed to want them there. I wanted nothing more than to make him as happy as he made me with every caress or kiss. "What are you thinking about?" John asked me as he stopped, his gaze meeting mine. "You suddenly seemed far away."

"I wasn't. I was thinking about you," I told him honestly, and I received a smile in return.

"I'm not sure if I should be insulted," John quipped, and I brought my arms down, circling them around him.

"I was thinking about you and how happy you make me."

John chuckled once again. "It's you who's made me happy." John wriggled his hips, and I felt his cock slide along mine. I couldn't stop a small gasp. "Like I said, you talk too much." John kissed away the rest of our words, and I wrapped my legs around his waist, wanting him so badly I could barely stand it.

John slithered down my body, his hair trailing over my skin. I held my breath, waiting for him. He kissed his way down my belly and then took me into his mouth, his lips slowly descending down my cock. I closed my eyes, mouth opening in a silent gasp as John took me deep. I thrust my hips and rested my hands on his head. Usually John stopped me, but this time he let me take control. John almost always needed to remain in control of our lovemaking, but not this time, and that gift drove me on. "Make love to me, John."

When he lifted his head, my cock slipped from his mouth, and I groaned at the loss even though I knew what was coming. What I didn't expect was for John to put his hand on my chest to still me before placing his knees on either side of my body. "John, are you…?" I gasped, and he nodded, his gaze blazing down at me. I tried to catch my breath as John reached to the bedside table. A small snick and John opened the bottle and poured the slick onto his fingers. I could hardly believe it when John placed the bottle back on the table and then his hand disappeared behind him. I wanted to twist myself into a pretzel so I could watch John sink his fingers inside himself, see his body as he took his own fingers inside. Instead, I saw John's eyes roll back into his head and heard his breath hitch. I wondered just what John was feeling at that moment. Had he ever done this before, or was I the first? I honestly didn't know. He'd never confided that part of himself to me, and while we'd talked of a great many things, this particular subject had never come up. He always seemed to need to be in control, and I was more than happy with that.

I felt John's grip around me, his slick fingers sliding up and down my shaft, and I throbbed with every touch. I heard a package open, and John rolled a condom down my length. Then John shifted, and he held me in position as I felt myself press to his opening. I had no control over our coupling—this was all John, even now—so I gripped his legs and did my best to revel in the sensation of having his body open up around me. "John, you don't have to," I said even as I said a silent prayer for him not to stop.

"I know," John whispered as he sank deeper. "You have given me more than anyone ever has, and I want to give this to you." He took me deeper and didn't stop until his butt rested against my hips. "I love you, Jerry."

"I love you too," I gasped as I arched my back, throwing my head back as he slowly lifted himself off me. Our eyes locked, and John reached out for me. I brought my hands up to meet his, and locked our fingers together. John rocked his hips, and I wanted to close my eyes, but didn't dare. The love that blazed in John's eyes drew me like a moth to flame. We were connected by body, hands, and heart. I could feel the last connection, just as strong and real as the others. Pulling John forward, I raised my legs to change the angle and began kissing John with everything I had.

When he straightened up again, I marveled at his glistening skin and strong torso, at his hair, cascading over his shoulders. Never in my life had I seen a more beautifully sexy sight. I felt John's weight shift. "No," I told him, and he stopped. "I want you just like this."

"But I thought you could...."

I shook my head. "Just like this. A strong and beautiful warrior, my warrior." John released my hands, and I ghosted my fingers down his skin. "You feel earth-shattering around me, like I'm inside a living furnace." John slowly began rocking his hips again, and this time he made small gasps and groans as we moved together. "You are my warrior, John, and you always will be."

"And you're mine!" John said as he clenched around me. I gasped and clamped my eyes closed, pressure already starting to build. "I used to think I was weak because I wanted this, wanted another man."

"No," I moaned as John took me hard and deep. "It takes strength to be yourself and to fight for what you want." I could not believe we were having this conversation while I was buried inside him, and yet it seemed so right and true. For some weird reason, it even made things hotter. We were sharing our hearts with each other just as we shared our bodies. "You are a warrior," I reiterated as John rolled his hips once again, his stomach muscles undulating like waves as my breath caught. I tried to stave off the impending release, but I had no control, John had stripped that away, so I gave myself over to it and let John drive the desire the way he always seemed to. "My warrior," I whispered, driving my hips upward as my control began to slip away. "I love you, my warrior," I gasped as my climax overtook me. I heard John gasp and then felt him reach his own release, coating my stomach with his searing climax.

I had no idea where the tears came from, but my eyes filled with them, and then they ran down my cheek. I felt John's weight shift, and he stroked my cheek, brushing away the tears before he cleaned my chest with his shirt. "You're my warrior," John whispered, and I gasped as I slipped from his body. "You fought for me and the kids when you hardly knew any of us." John shifted and settled on the bed next to me. I could hardly breathe, but that mattered very little as he nestled next to me. "You did that just because it was the right thing to do, and in the process, you captured my heart. My mother may have been testing you, but as far as I'm concerned, you passed the test a long time ago." John shifted and our gazes met. "No matter what anyone says or does, you are part of my family, just as much as Mato and Ichante. No one is going to take you away from me any more than they're going to be able to take those kids." John kissed me and then reached across to turn out the light. "I love you," John said in the darkness.

"I love you too," I told him and settled on the bed. "It seems strange to be talking like this in your parents' house," I confessed.

"This place has always been the heart of my family, so it seems right to me. You are family." I felt John roll over and tug me close. I closed my eyes and felt my lips curl into a smile.

"MATO, Ichante, come on down. We need to get ready to go," I called. Doors closed and little feet hurried down the stairs. John scooped Mato into his arms, and I caught Ichante as she reached the bottom of the stairs. "Your grandma is waiting for you, and we don't want to be late." Both kids were so different from the children I'd originally met months earlier when they were in foster care. Mato's hair was growing out and nearly reached to his collar, and Ichante's hair now reached her shoulders. But the physical changes were nothing compared to the inner light each of them had now. They laughed freely, played, ran, and even argued like normal kids. It was beautiful.

"Uncle Jerry, how long are we staying?" Mato asked, and I smiled. Since John's adoption of the kids had been finalized a month ago, both of them had taken to calling me Uncle Jerry. I'd never been called that by anyone before, and it still surprised me in the best way possible.

"Well, since Uncle Akecheta and Bryce helped me get that big assignment done early, we're going to stay a whole week, and you're going to play with your cousins, and you might even get to go camping." I looked at John, and he smiled. The man was amazing. He and Bryce had worked their butts off to get what the client wanted done months early.

"Can I go camping too?" Ichante asked.

"We'll all go, if that's what you want," I said, and I carried her toward the front door. I set her down, and she pulled her coat on as I heard a car pull up outside. "Uncle Bryce is here," I called, and the kids hurried to the door. Bryce had found himself alone for Thanksgiving. Percy had to work most of the week and was taking extra shifts. Bryce had been upset at first, but Percy had apparently explained that he would get time off at Christmas, but someone needed to work each holiday.

Bryce bounded into the house. "Get your things loaded into the van, and we'll get on the road," I told Bryce, and he hurried back outside.

"Is there anything we forgot?" John asked, and I shook my head. "I hope not. Otherwise there won't be room for us," John said.

I heard a vehicle pull into the drive, and I walked toward the front door. "Hey, guys," I called as Peter and Leonard got out of Leonard's truck. "I wasn't expecting you this morning." I quickly searched my memory to make sure I hadn't forgotten anything.

Leonard stepped up onto the porch. "We took a chance," he explained. "I just finished working on something for you, and I thought Thanksgiving was a good time to give it to you. Just wait here and we'll be right back." He looked excited as he hurried down the stairs, and I watched as Leonard and Peter walked around to the back of the truck. I heard the old tailgate squeak as Leonard lowered it. The door behind me opened, and I turned as John stepped out of the house.

"The kids are ready whenever you are," he told me, and I nodded to him before watching as Leonard and Peter carried a long wooden bench up the stairs. They set it against the house near the swing.

"This bench was one of the projects your grandfather had started but didn't finish," Leonard told me, and he and Peter stepped back. "All I did was make the few final pieces, put it together, and finish it."

I stepped forward and ran my hand over the carving of vines that ran along the back. "It's beautiful," I said softly.

"Your grandfather did all the carving. He was very talented," Leonard said from behind me, and I turned and hugged him tight. "I thought you'd like to have it."

"Thank you," I said softly, hugging him and then Peter before sitting down on the bench. I probably should have had a coat on, but it didn't matter. I ran my hand over the smooth arm of the bench and tried my best not to blubber like a girl. It felt strange, but as I closed my eyes, I could almost feel my grandfather working in his shop, shaping and sanding the wood by hand. In some way it was sort of like Leonard had given me a piece of my grandfather back. "Thank you so much," I said, and then I heard the door open. Mato and Ichante rushed over, both of them joining me on the bench. John lifted Ichante onto his lap and then sat down next to me, one arm winding around my waist. *My family*.

"Can we go to Gramma's now?" Mato asked. I laughed and stood up, lifting Mato into my arms. I said good-bye to both Leonard and Peter with Mato resting his head on my shoulder, and I used him as a shield so no one would see the tears. I waved as Leonard and Peter pulled away, and then I carried Mato to the van, making sure he was secured in his seat while John got Ichante ready and made sure everything was loaded. I checked the house one last time, leaving by the front door to take another look at the bench, and then we were off.

The kids played car games with Bryce until they fell asleep, and I drove until my legs tingled. We stopped to eat in Wall, and then John drove the rest of the way to his mother's. As I'd expected, the entire family was there, the yard filled with kids. As soon as the car stopped, Mato and Ichante were out of their seats. Once John opened the door, they hurried out. I watched, standing next to John, as they ran and played with the others. "So what's on the agenda for the week?"

"Well," I said, checking my watch, "we have about an hour to unload our things and then we need to leave. Grandma is going to watch the kids while we're gone." I leaned against John for a few seconds and then we got to work.

Kiya met us at the door and showed us to our rooms. After quickly unpacking, we met in the yard and got back in the van. "We'll see you boys when you get back," Kiya said, leaning into John's open window to give him yet another hug. Once she stepped back, I started the engine and followed John's directions to the community center. When I'd parked, John led me inside and down a hallway before pushing open a door.

The room was set up with a dozen tables, with a computer sitting on each one. This wasn't some fancy lab where all equipment was identical and the latest available. Each of the computers was older, and no two were alike, but that didn't matter. John and I had secured each one as a donation and then worked to refurbish them before sending them on. "So what are we doing again?" Bryce asked.

"John is teaching a beginner's computer class, and we're going to assist him," I told him. "We've been arranging for donated computers to go to school kids," I explained as I began going through the room turning on the machines. "The response with donations has been so great that we're offering computers to adults as well. All they need to do is take a few classes so we can show them the basics, and then we'll give them each their own computer."

"So this is what you guys have been doing on those weekends you disappear," Bryce said as he gave us a hand.

"Yup," I answered happily as we finished setting up the room. When I'd started, I'd had no idea just how positively the program would be accepted, but the response had been amazing. We'd just finished setting up when people began arriving, and soon each station was full and John started the class. The students ranged from younger people to grandparents, each as excited as the next. They kept all three of us hopping with their questions, and by the time the class was ending, the questions were still coming. Bryce sat between two people and worked with both of them while John and I helped the rest. Once the class was over, John handed each of the students a laptop and received a grateful smile and a thank-you from each one. One woman hugged all three of us before saying that now she'd be able to e-mail her grandchildren in Omaha.

"This really made a difference," Bryce observed as we closed up the lab.

"I think so," John said. "The people at the school have said the computers we've sent for the students have made a world of difference." He turned out the light, and we walked out of the center, saying good-bye at the desk before walking across the parking lot to the van. "Sometimes I wish other things could change as easily," John noted as he pulled open the driver's door. I knew he was talking about the foster care situation with Native American children, but the publicity from John's case had had an effect, though whether it was temporary or lasting had yet to be determined.

"We do what we can to make things better," I told John, and he settled in his seat and leaned over for a kiss, which I gave readily. "And we're doing what we can."

"This is all because of you," John told me, and I thought he was going to kiss me again, but instead he started the engine and drove back to his mother's without saying anything more. When we arrived the yard was quiet, but inside, the house was full to bursting, with Kiya cooking up a storm. Bryce got tugged into one of the rooms by Mato, and I got taken by the hand by John and led upstairs to our room.

"I take it there's something you want to say. You've been quiet since we left the community center," I said as John closed the bedroom door.

"I've been thinking. Somehow you make a difference for everyone around you."

"I didn't do anything special," I said.

"Yes, you did," John corrected. "You give of yourself every day, from taking care of me and the kids, to helping here, to twisting arms to get computer donations, and I want to do something just for you." I was looking around, wondering just what John had in mind, when I saw him go down on one knee.

"John," I murmured.

"I'm not going to ask you to marry me, but I am going to ask you to take me as your partner for the rest of our lives." John's gaze met mine, and I gently tugged him back to his feet.

"Yes, my warrior," I told him as I drew him into a kiss.

# STORIES FROM THE RANGE

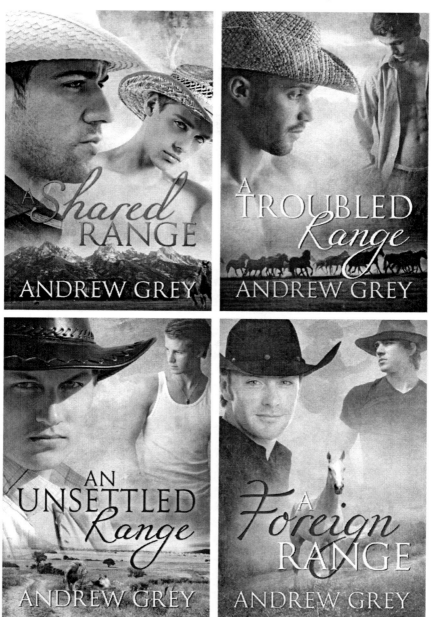

http://www.dreamspinnerpress.com

# BOTTLED UP STORIES

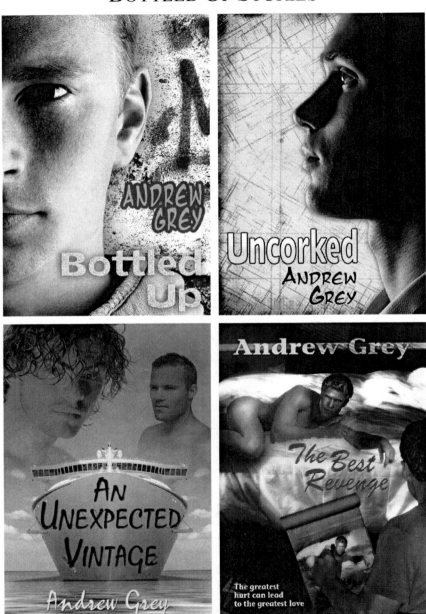

http://www.dreamspinnerpress.com

# LOVE MEANS…

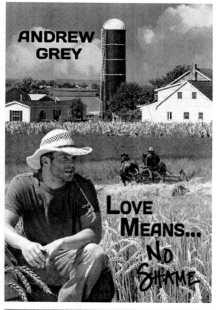

http://www.dreamspinnerpress.com

# Now in French, Italian, and Spanish

# THE ART SERIES

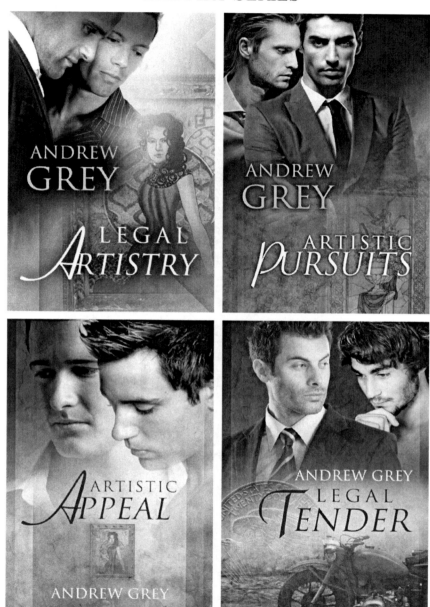

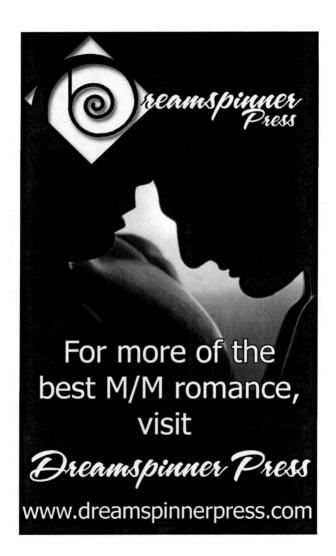

CPSIA information can be obtained at www.ICGtesting.com
Printed in the USA
LVOW100415250912

300178LV00001B/88/P